THE KEEPER OF THE ELEMENTS

Copyright © 2022 by Esther Allen

All rights reserved. No part of this book may be reproduced or used in any manner without written permission of the copyright owner except for the use of quotations in a book review.

Book design by Simona Pedrali Noy

ISBN: 9798353474586 (paperback)

The
Keeper
of the
Elements

Esther Allen

Index

Chapter One — 11

Chapter Two — 19

Chapter Three — 29

Chapter Four — 37

Chapter Five — 53

Chapter Six — 73

Chapter Seven — 89

Chapter Eight — 111

Chapter Nine — 133

Chapter Ten — 147

Chapter Eleven — 163

Chapter Twelve — 187

Epilogue — 203

For my sister Eli,
who helped me find my passion for writing.

CHAPTER ONE

Prophecies

Xander entered the dull interior of the chamber. He shifted his weight, and his long, spiked tail brushed against the floor as he looked around the room with contempt. Xander snorted, causing puffs of smoke to curl out of his slit-like nostrils.

"Shut," said Xander shortly, his harsh voice penetrating the silence.

The door closed as if by the hand of an invisible creature, and the room was instantly engulfed in darkness.

Xander walked to the middle of the chamber. An ominous creaking ensued as the floor started lowering. Xander's large, scaly wings brushed against the stone walls and he dug his claws deep into the soft carpet. As the floor lowered the last few inches, Xander released his claws and slid into the tunnel-like entrance before him.

He entered into a long hallway, the walls of which were engraved with carvings of the past. On one wall, the details of past dragons had faded, replaced by cobwebs and dust. Another wall depicted a boy. Xander's sharp teeth bared; the boy was the Keeper, or the Destined One —as hopeful people called him. The boy was prophesied to destroy Xander's master, but prophecies were foolish —and they could be undone.

Xander looked away from the walls as the hall ended. Before him was an arched door. As he drew closer, the door opened, the hinges creaking in indignation. With a deep breath that caused puffs of curling smoke to escape from his nostrils, Xander stepped over the threshold.

The chamber was dark, except for a few lit torches adorning the walls. Xander's long shadow stretched across the door as it closed.

A throne faced Xander. It was made of pure silver, except for flecks of gold over the back of the throne. The armrests had queer engravings, not actual images, rather curls and undulating lines.

A raven was perched on the throne. One of its beady eyes regarded Xander with suspicion. Its sharp claws were clasped around the silver armrest.

Through an open window high in the wall, the pearly moonlight bathed the throne in silver. The gold shimmered like the crystals of a rock cave.

Lord Invictius stepped from the shadows, and Xander bowed his head. Invictius' eyes were like dark pits, filled with black fire. The shadows clung to him as if drawn to his presence.

"Xander," acknowledged Invictius, his cloak lifting off the dust-ridden floor of its own accord.

"Lord Invictius," said Xander, bowing his scaly head.

"You asked for this meeting. See to it that our time does not go to waste." Lord Invictius reposed himself upon the throne.

"Of course, my lord. I have found the boy again."

CHAPTER ONE

"Where?" asked Invictius.

His voice was cold. Poised.

"Nolman's Realm. In a village to the east, surrounded by woods."

Invictius nodded thoughtfully.

"Is it protected?"

"No… my lord. It is a… solitary village."

"Very well. Onyx will take care of this matter."

Xander met Invictius' dark eyes with shock.

"Lord, Onyx is too dangerous! We need him alive! She will kill the humans and then there will be another war between–"

"Silence."

Lord Invictius did not say it loudly. The way he glared at Xander was enough.

"If they had not taken Morgana I would have used her. Onyx is my second hunter. She will be given this task. Is that understood?" Invictius' black eyes regarded Xander disdainfully.

"But–"

"Remember, dragon! Remember what I did to your village. I trust you do not have the urge to go the same way."

Xander would have paled, if blood ran through his veins. The memories of that place were brief, but vivid. The memories of it being frozen down were the worst of them all.

"Yes, my lord," said Xander with a bow of his head.

"I am relieved you have enough sense to agree," said Invictius, smiling grimly. "Now, turning to other matters... is she in place?"

"Yes."

Invictius nodded with satisfaction. The first parts of the plan were moving perfectly.

"You may go now, Xander."

With one last bow, Xander backed out of the chamber as gracefully as his large wings would allow. The doors swung closed in his face, and he turned away with a soft snort.

* * *

Once the dragon's footsteps had faded out of earshot, the raven flew down from the rafters and landed gracefully on his forearm. Her head lifted elegantly to meet Invictius' dark eyes.

"Go, Corvina. Call Onyx."

Corvina bowed her head and spread her wings. With one last glance at Invictius, she took off, using the window as her door.

Lord Invictius watched her departing back and settled himself back onto his throne. He had been looking for the boy –the Keeper– ever since he had heard of the prophecy. If Xander was mistaken about his whereabouts, well... that was another matter.

CHAPTER ONE

The familiar beat of Corvina's wings caused Invictius to look up. She landed on Invictius' shoulder just as he heard Onyx's voice.

The heavy doors opened, their rusting hinges groaning in response. Two guards clad in armor marched through the entrance, holding Onyx between them.

Onyx. A curious creature. She seemed to hate him, though he had rescued her from the flames of her destruction. She was so similar to humans in all the worst possible ways.

She held her wings wide open behind her, her pride and power displayed in that simple gesture. The feathers of her wings were black, yet shimmered with slight traces of silver.

Onyx had high, sharp cheekbones that accentuated her large, silver eyes filled with hatred for him. Her long, dark hair extended past her shoulders, hiding her pointed elf-ears. Her face was as pale as death itself, and she was wearing a dress that was frayed at the hem. The sleeves had been torn, and her slender hands were chained in shackles that bit into her skin.

They had been placed there to stop her from destroying everything she touched. Although they did not always work.

Onyx smiled and inclined her head in a bow.

"You called me. My lord?"

She lifted her eyes to his as if mocking him.

"Yes, I have a task for you," said Lord Invictius, standing up.

"Of course. Why else would you have taken me out of my beloved prison?"

"Don't you dare speak to me like that," said Invictius icily, stepping forward.

"I will speak to you as I like." Onyx replied coldly, her eyes suddenly blazing. "You are not worthy of respect."

There was a pause in which Invictius noticed the guards glance uneasily at each other.

"Enough," said Invictius with a tone of finality. "I have a task for you, and you will carry it out, understood?"

"Yes." Her wings widened.

"There is a boy in the Nolman's Realm. I want you to bring him to me."

"The Keeper?" asked Onyx with a small smile.

"The Hunters will go with you," said Invictius, ignoring her question.

Onyx's smile fell, and her eyes burned with anger.

"I can track the boy by myself," snarled Onyx. "I do not need a pack of wild wolves to help me."

"They know the forests," said Invictius calmly, but threateningly. "If you do not go with them, I will not let you out."

Onyx didn't say anything. She put all she had to say in her piercing gaze.

CHAPTER ONE

"That is all. You may leave."

Two guards grasped Onyx's arms, and she glared at Invictius as they started leading her out. Invictius met Onyx's eyes, and saw the hatred burning in them as the doors creaked shut.

the Keeper of the Elements

CHAPTER TWO

Whispers

Jason lay awake, staring at the ceiling. The moonlight coming through his window illuminated his face with an eerie glow.

He sighed and sat up, annoyed with himself for not being asleep. He got out of bed and left his room. As he passed through the hallway and started going downstairs, he heard voices. Whispers.

After a moment of hesitation, Jason leaned forward and tried to discern what they were saying.

"I will look for the boy," said a feminine voice, "you and your pack stay outside, and if you find him do not kill him. The master wants him alive."

"Yes, Onyx."

Jason could hardly distinguish the words. The voice sounded more like a growl than anything.

He heard light footsteps enter the kitchen, and his breath caught as shivers of fear rolled over him. He was breathing hard and crept up the stairs, to safety.

Jason rushed to his aunt's room.

She was awake and dressed in a long, black cloak. Her kind, oval-shaped face was bent over a backpack and her wavy auburn hair fell over her shoulders. Jason caught only a glimpse of the objects inside before she zipped it closed.

"Skylar?"

She looked up at his words, her blue eyes gleaming in the dark.

"Do you remember what I told you?" asked Skylar, her voice urgent.

"Yes."

Years ago, she had told him to always have a bag prepared with clothes and boots. The bag was back in his room, though. Under his bed.

"Do you have the bag prepared?"

Jason nodded.

"Good. Put this cloak on."

Jason slipped it on. The inside felt comfortable and soft, the outside strange and scaly. Two large pockets were on either side of the cloak.

"What will it do?"

"It's fireproof, it will protect you if they bring dragons," said Skylar, checking outside the window.

"Dragons?" asked Jason, his mind filled with thoughts of fire breathing, winged lizards.

CHAPTER TWO

"I will explain later, Jason, when we get somewhere safe."

She was looking under the bed, obviously looking for something.

"But... they're real?"

"I'm sorry Jason, there is no time. I promise, once we get out of here, I will explain everything."

Skylar grabbed something from under the bed and stood up. She held a long wooden staff that bore glowing purple engravings. A violet orb was suspended between two elegantly interlaced branches.

Jason gazed at it speechless, but the creak of a door shook him out of his reverie.

"They're here," said Skylar.

She closed her eyes, and Jason noticed her hold on the staff tighten.

A spark shot out of the orb, and soon a dark tunnel-like hole appeared and started to grow. Jason stepped back as it started expanding. In mere seconds, it had grown large enough for Skylar to fit through.

She took a deep breath and opened her eyes. Relief was etched in the lines across her face.

"Get inside, hurry," said Skylar with a worn but reassuring smile.

She gave Jason a backpack, and he slipped it on. It was made of the same material as the cloak.

Jason looked at her worriedly.

"I'll be alright, don't worry." She hugged him tight, and Jason's fear vanished.

"Go."

With a last glance at her face and a deep breath, he jumped.

Jason felt his stomach tighten. He was spinning around so fast it felt like a whirlpool. With the sound of crunching snow, he hit the ground and felt cold snow on his face and in his mouth.

He felt dizzy, but safe. The absolute silence around him was startling, yet calming.

Jason opened his eyes and realized that there was no sign of his aunt. Naked trees stood above him like hunters bent upon their prey. The full moon was visible over the treetops, casting silver light as far as Jason could see.

Jason was breathing hard. There shouldn't be snow. It didn't snow in autumn. Where was he? Where was Skylar?

Jason saw a shadow, and heard a soft thud as someone landed in the snow.

Jason rushed forward. It was Skylar, but something was wrong. Her eyes were closed and her face was pale. Jason felt her pulse; it was going irregularly fast. He opened the backpack and started rummaging inside, desperately looking for something that could

CHAPTER TWO

help her. He stopped as he heard the soft crunch of snow. Jason looked around the clearing, but there was no-one in sight.

The sound came again, this time closer, but still Jason saw no-one. He looked back at Skylar. Something grabbed his arm. He kicked at it, its grip slackened and finally broke.

A girl materialized on the ground in front of Jason. Jason stepped back at her sudden appearance, but she didn't move.

Her dark, curly hair framed her jawline, and glowed red where it caught in the moonlight. She wore a black and red outfit that Jason imagined a hunter would wear. It had a lot of belts and a couple of straps. Her black trousers looked like a slightly more elegant version of combat trousers, held up by a bright red leather belt. Jason counted at least ten pockets, each of them outlined with red stitches. She wore a sleeveless wolf fur coat that complemented the rest of her outfit and sturdy black leather boots. Her eyes were focused on Jason. They glowed red in the dark.

Jason stepped back; he wasn't ready for this. He must be imagining it.

"I'm here to help," said the girl, getting to her feet.

"Who are you?" asked Jason.

"I'm Ember. You can trust me."

Jason was hesitant and looked at his aunt. He took a step towards Skylar, but Ember didn't move. She watched him with a curious expression, almost as though she were testing him.

Jason hurried forward and knelt down beside his aunt.

He sighed in relief when he noticed that her pulse was regular and the color was coming back to her cheeks.

Jason turned back to the girl. Ember hadn't moved.

"Why are you here?" asked Jason, standing up. He was slightly annoyed to find that the girl was taller than him.

"I need to bring you somewhere safe," replied Ember. She spoke as though she had been told exactly what to say.

"Where are you going to take me?"

"Somewhere Invictius' forces cannot find you," she said, hesitating at his name.

"Who is Invictius?"

She seemed surprised by the question, but masked it with a calm expression.

"Perhaps it's best if I wake Skylar up first."

"How do you know her name?"

"I..." Ember sighed and paused. "Listen, just let me wake her up, and we can explain everything."

"I don't even know who you are."

"But Skylar does. I can wake her up, I just need a moment."

"Jason. She's trustworthy."

CHAPTER TWO

Jason glanced at Skylar, who was sitting up and smiling at Ember. Relief flooded through Jason, and he knelt back down beside Skylar.

"You're okay," said Jason.

Skylar embraced Jason and got to her feet.

"Ember. It's been so long," said Skylar as she hugged Ember.

"Skylar," said Ember, returning the embrace.

"Oh, you do know her," said Jason, feeling strangely out of place.

"I trained Ember. I am glad that you two did not end up fighting," said Skylar, turning to Jason.

Ember smiled with a twinkle in her eyes.

"Where are we?" asked Jason.

"The Realm of Sorcerers," said Skylar, as she picked up Jason's pack from the ground and handed it to him.

"Realm?" asked Jason, his mind momentarily going through a million things at once.

Skylar hesitated.

"Perhaps I should explain later. When we're safe," said Skylar, her brow furrowed. "Ember, is Morpheus at the castle?"

"Yes."

"Wait, castle?" asked Jason. "What castle?"

"All right," said Skylar with a sigh. "I suppose I should explain this now. Our world is just a piece of the universe around us, Jason. There are actually seven main Realms in which creatures and people live. Our world, the one you knew, is called the Nolman's Realm. This is the Sorcerer's Realm, and the Realm we are going to is called the Wizard's Realm. There we will meet Morpheus."

"How is that possible?" asked Jason.

"It's not safe right now, Jason. Once we're safe, and rested up, I will explain everything. I promise."

Jason sighed.

"All right."

Skylar smiled, looking as weary as Jason had ever seen her.

"Ember."

Ember nodded and flicked her wrist. For a moment there was a small fire in the palm of her hand. As the fire disappeared, it was replaced by an engraved wooden staff. The staff had strange words engraved on its surface. A red stone was suspended between the majestically interwoven branches.

"Sudden teleportation or portal?" asked Ember.

"Sudden; we can't have anyone following us."

Ember nodded.

CHAPTER TWO

Skylar laid her bag on the ground and zipped it open. She pulled out a pair of sturdy-looking shoes in Jason's size.

"Put them on, please, Jason," said Skylar. "You can change at the castle."

Jason quickly pulled them on and Skylar straightened up again.

"There. Time to leave," said Skylar.

Ember nodded and closed her eyes. Jason's skin started prickling and then his vision suddenly went dark.

the Keeper of the Elements

CHAPTER THREE

The Castle

When Jason opened his eyes, he was in a completely different place. It was day here, and the sun beat down ferociously. The trees were made of crystal. Their diamond-like leaves chimed in the wind. A clump of purple flowers stood under each tree, as if feeding on the shade the trees provided.

He looked to his right to see Skylar. She smiled reassuringly at him and glanced at Ember.

Ember was observing their surroundings, her staff at the ready.

"No one in sight," said Ember.

Jason glanced around and realised Ember was right. There was no sight, nor sound, of any other living creature. The silence was overwhelming.

"Where are we?" Skylar asked Ember.

"Five minutes away from the castle," answered Ember.

Skylar nodded and Ember flicked her wrist. Her staff disappeared in a flash of crimson flames.

Skylar stood up and adjusted her backpack. "Let's get going then."

Skylar glanced up at the sky for a moment, then nodded to herself and began leading them through the forest. After a while the trees started to be few and far between, and before long, the castle lay before them.

Skylar led the way through a bustling street of villagers. After following the road for some time, they arrived right in front of the stone wall which ran around the castle. Skylar approached the gate. Two guards stood on either side of it.

"Don't take another step," warned the guard, as Skylar came closer.

Jason was certain he would be true to his word. Both guards held staffs much the same as Ember's and Skylar's, although theirs shone as though made of metal instead of wood.

"We're actually here to see Morpheus," said Skylar.

"The King's advisor?" said the other guard.

"Yes," said Skylar.

"Can you confirm that he has invited you?" said the guard.

"Yes, I have a message from him."

Skylar flicked her wrist, causing her staff to appear in her hand. She touched the staff's stone, which glowed for a second. As the light died away, shimmering letters appeared in the air before the guards. The letters were completely foreign to Jason, but the guards read the message and then nodded. One of the guards

CHAPTER THREE

touched his staff to the gate, and the doors slowly began opening.

They entered a beautiful garden full of bright silver trees surrounded by tiny shimmering fairies that hovered around them. The grass was a delicate lilac, adding an element of surrealism to the garden.

"That wasn't too hard," said Ember, as they walked across the castle grounds.

Skylar smiled, but as they passed some other guards conducting their rounds in the gardens, her smile vanished. The guards' expressions were stony and cold, and the metal of their staves glinted in the sun.

Jason felt like hiding when he saw them. He noticed Ember looking at them with a cold look on her face.

"I still haven't forgiven them for hunting me down," said Ember, once they were out of earshot.

"Morpheus still has not forgiven you for stealing the dragon egg," said Skylar softly with a glance at Ember.

Ember pretended not to have heard her.

The gardens were huge, and it took some time for them to reach the doors of the castle. The doors were made of thick oak wood that shone with the remnants of thousands of ancient enchantments. Golden spirals engraved on the doors conveyed a sense of majesty.

Skylar tapped the wood with her staff. For a second, nothing happened, but after a moment, the doors creaked open as if by magic.

Jason gasped as he stepped inside the castle.

Brightly colored trees grew out of the high ceiling, creating the illusion that they were walking upside down. There were crystal windows that were too high to reach, but bathed the hall in golden light. Tapestries woven out of gold adorned the walls and sparkled in the light from the windows. Silver suits of armor were lined up against the wall, sharp swords held in their armored hands. The floor was decorated with a long carpet that had mythical animals woven into it.

Jason barely noticed Skylar and Ember walking ahead of him as he took in the beauty and royalty of the hall, but once he did, he hurried to catch up with them.

The rest of the hall was just as amazing as the entrance. If anything, the enchantments grew more incredible. The creatures on the carpet started moving under Jason, and a purple dragon woven inside the carpet started flying after him, snapping at his heels.

Finally, they approached a pair of large, mahogany doors. Skylar tapped the wood with her staff, just as she had done before, and the doors slowly opened, revealing a large room.

A stone fireplace was situated at the end of the room. A portrait of a stern-looking man hung over it. A glass chandelier hung above the room, where it twinkled as though moving, despite the lack of any breeze. Two velvet couches faced each other and a small, crystal table stood between them. Wooden doors faced each other on opposite walls. The walls were made of plain oak, which gave a warm, earthy ambience to the room. A man was sitting on one of the couches. He was facing the fire and held in his hand a glass of swirling, golden liquid.

CHAPTER THREE

"Enter," said the man.

Skylar led the way inside the room.

"Hello, Morpheus," said Skylar.

The man turned to her. He had sparkling blue eyes that glanced at Jason. For a moment, Jason saw the grim look in his eyes, but the next moment his lips curled in a soft, almost-welcoming smile. His nose was as thin and sharp as a dagger. A wispy goatee adorned his jutting chin.

He laid his glass on the table and stood up, his height becoming more obvious as he towered over them. He bowed his head to Skylar, a sweeping gesture that made Jason feel oddly out of place. The man's emerald robes fluttered around him.

"Hello," said Ember, her expression cold and hostile.

"Hello, Ember," said Morpheus, his blue eyes observing her with barely masked condescension.

She nodded once to acknowledge him, then looked away. There was an awkward pause, and the sense of bad blood in the air.

"Morpheus, this is Jason," said Skylar, her smile slightly forced.

Morpheus met Jason's eyes, causing him to feel observed and uncomfortable. Finally, Morpheus bowed his head towards him.

"Welcome to the castle."

Jason nodded. Morpheus gave him the creeps.

"How was your journey?" Morpheus asked Skylar, though his eyes lingered on Jason for a moment longer.

"Tiring, but, fine, I suppose."

"Excellent! Would you like to be shown to your chambers? The journey must have been simply exhausting, and the time difference will have affected you."

Skylar nodded.

"That would be much appreciated."

Morpheus gestured with his hand and his staff appeared. It was slightly different than any staff Jason had seen so far: the wood bore traces of gold, and though it spiraled together, the stone suspended between the branches shone golden instead of red or purple.

Morpheus thumped the staff on the ground. A few seconds later, a small, person-like creature entered through one of the doors.

She wore a cream-coloured cloak with a golden sash, and was barely taller than Jason's midriff. She looked thin and underfed, and her tan skin simply added to this impression. Her eyes were a pale pink and unnaturally large. She had sharp ears and a small, pointy nose.

"Willow, please escort Jason to the east tower."

Willow nodded her head and looked up at Jason. He looked at Skylar, who nodded at him encouragingly, but with a worried smile. With a last glance at Morpheus and Ember, Jason was escorted out of the room.

CHAPTER THREE

* * *

As the door closed behind Jason, Morpheus turned back to Skylar.

"Do you really think he is the Destined One?" asked Morpheus, his polite smile gone, his eyes dead-serious.

"Why else would Invictius be searching for him?" said Skylar.

"Perhaps he's actually looking for you," said Morpheus.

"I don't even know if he remembers me," said Skylar softly.

There was a moment of silence at that.

"Well, if Invictius is after him, then I think he should be moved somewhere safe," proposed Ember.

Morpheus looked at her coldly.

"The castle is the safest place for the boy."

"Really?" said Ember, her red eyes flashing with impatience. "Do you really think so? Morgana is in the dungeons below us, and Onyx is hunting Jason. If Onyx were to free Morgana this could quickly become the most dangerous place for Jason."

Morpheus had no words to counteract her argument.

"Ember, calm down," said Skylar. "As for you," she turned to Morpheus. "Can't you put the past behind you? She stole the dragon egg for a good reason. She saved my life! Surely you can admit that the best thing to do is to forgive and move on."

Morpheus looked at her in silent fury.

"Now, we need to call the Guardians. It will help if we have more opinions," said Skylar.

Ember nodded but kept her gaze on Morpheus. Skylar could see that he was unnerved by the deep scarlet of her eyes. Her eyes always changed color when she was angry or feeling a strong emotion. Morpheus still hadn't gotten accustomed to it.

"I don't want you two talking to Jason about these things though; he isn't ready yet," said Skylar.

There was a pause, and Morpheus turned his eyes away from Ember.

"Very well," said Morpheus a bit stiffly.

Ember nodded, and her eyes slowly changed back to hazel, though in the light it looked like there was still a faint gleam of scarlet.

Skylar, nodded. "Thank you. Please announce a meeting of the Guardians, Morpheus, and make sure no-one approaches him about the prophecy."

"Very well," said Morpheus.

"Now, if you two don't mind, I would like to have a moment to myself. Where are my chambers, Morpheus?"

"East wing, as usual."

"Goodnight, then," said Skylar. And with that, she left the room.

CHAPTER FOUR

Burnt Feathers

The room Jason was to stay in seemed larger than his entire house, and certainly much more majestic. The trees painted on the walls were so realistic, they emanated a sense of enchantment. A window made of crystal occupied an entire wall and a sparkling chandelier, made out of gold, hung over the centre of the room. An oak wardrobe, with golden symbols painted over it, took up another wall. The far wall had two large dressers pushed against it, with a four-poster bed in between them. A large emerald lamp lay on one of the dressers.

Willow hurried to open the large window, and with the fresh air came an oddly pleasant scent. Jason sighed and felt his muscles relax. He felt safer than he had all morning.

But then he remembered all Skylar had told him so far. He simply couldn't understand the fact that the world he had known was just a small part of the universe, a tiny part in fact. And yet he had already traveled to two Realms.

Jason was shaken out of his thoughts by the sound of a polite cough. Willow was looking up at his face. Her small hands clasped together respectfully.

"Oh. Yes?" said Jason, having forgotten all about her.

"Would you like some food, sir? We can prepare something of your choice."

"No, thank you, I'd just like to sleep."

"All right, sir, I will tell the rest of the servants to leave you be."

With a last glance around to make sure all was as it should be, Willow hurried out of the room.

Jason made his way to the bed, and wearily took off the fireproof cloak. He threw himself onto the bed and just like that, slipped into his dreams.

* * *

Jason gradually woke up, a gentle breeze blowing his ink-black hair in his eyes. He sat up, opening his eyes as he did so. He looked towards the window. The night was ending, and the sun was slowly rising over the horizon. The stars were fading and slowly being replaced by dark blue sky.

Jason got out of bed, realizing he had slept for a full day. The room had grown uncomfortably cold during the night, and Jason quickly walked across the cold floor and closed the window. His skin prickled at the change of temperature.

Jason turned around and was about to take a step towards his bed when he saw a silhouette in the corner. He froze, watching it.

After a moment or two, a sudden light flooded the room.
Jason stepped back at the sight of Ember standing there staring at him. She had replaced her fur coat with a long, black cloak that had red webs running along it. She held her staff in her hand, a soft red glow emanating from the stone.

CHAPTER FOUR

"You scared me," said Jason.

Ember didn't say anything. She just looked at him.

"What are you doing here?"

"Just waiting for you to wake up."

"Did you sleep at all?"

Ember cast him a strange look.

"I slept enough."

"Okay, well, you creeped me out."

The corner of Ember's mouth twitched in amusement.

"Why are you waiting anyway?" asked Jason.

"We wanted to give you a tour of the castle. Skylar is in the dining room waiting for you."

"I thought she was going to explain everything."

"That will have to wait. She will explain everything tomorrow if she can," said Ember, with no further explanation.

Jason saw a flash of crimson in her eyes, as if warning him, but she quickly turned away before Jason could be sure.

"I'll call Willow to bring you a proper cloak. What color do you want?"

"Uh, any is fine."

"All right, Willow will arrive soon."

With that, Ember walked to the door, opened it, and with a last glance at Jason, left.

Jason felt slightly confused at Ember's behavior, but sighed and turned to the wardrobe. Jason pulled open the doors of the wardrobe, and simply stared at the hundreds of clothes inside before quickly changing into a plain shirt and a pair of trousers. He then pulled on the boots he had thrown aside the night before and waited.

Before long, Willow arrived, holding a cloak that matched Jason's eyes. It was made of royal-blue silk and had golden lines that began at the sleeves and ended at the neck.

Jason quickly slipped it on and noticed the large pockets on the interior that had fur lining the inside. It fit him perfectly, and was comfortable and soft. The sleeves encased his arms perfectly. The cloak's hem barely touched the floor, and didn't drag behind him.

"If you will follow me, sir."

Willow hurried out of the room, her short legs practically running. Jason followed.

Before long, they had arrived at the dining room, and Willow hurried off, muttering something about 'rooms to be cleaned and food to be cooked'.

The doors opened before Jason even had a chance to touch them. He took a step back in surprise as the dining room was slowly revealed.

CHAPTER FOUR

A long table took up the middle of the room, big enough to seat twenty people at least. The table was set with various fruits and snacks. A crystal chandelier hung over the table, and the candles were lit, filling the room with a soft light. On the far wall, there was a fireplace which, had the table not been in the way, would have been in full view.

Morpheus stood up as Jason entered the room. He held his golden staff in one hand, causing him to look imposing and regal. Skylar and Ember simply turned to look at him. Jason nervously made his way across the room and sat down beside Skylar, who smiled at him in greeting. Ember looked at him over her mug filled with steaming hot chocolate.

Morpheus sat back down. He had a queer smile that made Jason feel strange.

"We thought you'd like a tour of the castle. Have some breakfast, and we'll start immediately," said Skylar, her own plate looking as though it hadn't been touched.

"How do I order?"

"Just say what you would like to eat, and it will appear."

"Okay," said Jason slowly. "Then I would like some oatmeal."

Immediately, a steaming bowl of oatmeal appeared before him. It smelled wonderfully fresh, as if it had just been cooked and had come off the stove mere seconds ago. At the same time, a silver spoon materialized next to Jason's right arm.

"Wow," said Jason, surprised.

"Eat up," said Ember, sipping her hot chocolate.

Jason started eating, and, before he knew it, the bowl was empty. He felt pleasantly full and ready to start what would undoubtedly be a very unusual day. Once Jason had finished eating, Morpheus stood up.

"Let us go then, there is much to see."

Skylar rose from her seat, soon followed by Jason and Ember.

Morpheus led them through one of the many doors out of the dining room. They entered a hallway. Torches on the walls lit the way for them. After a while, they came to a door which swung open as they approached.

The inside of the room was bustling with creatures that looked just like Willow, bringing food to tables all over the room. In one corner, there was another door which the creatures came in and out from.

"This is the kitchen. These sprites take care of the cleaning and cooking of the castle," said Morpheus.

The sprites looked up at his voice, but immediately went back to work when they saw that he wasn't calling for any of them.

Jason watched them for a bit and noticed that the sprites coming through the door often had food in their hands and placed it on the table. They then scuttered back through the door.

They watched the sprites for a while, but after a few minutes Morpheus closed the door.

"We shouldn't bother them too long, they have work to do. What other rooms can we show him?" Morpheus looked at Skylar.

CHAPTER FOUR

"What about—"

"The dungeons!" said Ember.

"I suppose that would be entertaining," said Skylar hesitantly.

"Absolutely not, the dungeons are horrible. I forbid that we go there," said Morpheus.

"Fine," said Ember bitterly.

"What if," said Skylar cautiously, avoiding Ember's piercing stare, "we go to the Star Room?"

"Perfect, it is a good educational room," said Morpheus.

"All right then, it is decided," said Skylar, ignoring the look of resentment on Ember's face.

"Let's use the wall," said Skylar. "The Room is on the other side of the castle."

"All right, I suppose it wouldn't hurt."

Morpheus closed the kitchen door and touched the wall. Glowing words —made of letters that Jason didn't recognize— appeared on the wall. Morpheus chose a word, and Jason felt a cold prickling sensation travel through his body. Jason felt light-headed and noticed that they had appeared in another part of the castle. He leaned on the wall for a few seconds as he regained his balance.

"Are you all right?" asked Skylar as he steadied himself.

"Yeah, I'm fine."

Skylar smiled, but some anxiety remained in her eyes.

"All right, this way," said Morpheus.

He led them through the hall, and Jason looked up at the ceiling when he noticed the glittering stars in the corner of his eyes.

He felt a hand on his shoulder and glanced at Skylar, who was looking at Morpheus, who was reading glowing letters that hung in the air before him.

"I need to go," said Morpheus abruptly.

"Why?" asked Skylar, reading the message he had received.

"The king needs me. Continue with the tour; I will return soon. Understood?" Morpheus slipped past them with the air of someone that had something urgent to attend to.

He disappeared before he had reached the end of the hall.

"That was strange," said Ember, looking at the spot where he had disappeared.

Skylar didn't answer, but her eyes remained transfixed to where he had vanished.

"Let's keep going with the tour," said Ember.

Skylar nodded and turned back to the door. Ember pushed the door open and entered the room, closely followed by Jason and Skylar.

Jason gasped as he took in the wonder of the room. It was shaped like a circular dome. The walls of the Star Room were enchanted

CHAPTER FOUR

to display the stars of the night. The ceiling was enchanted to do the same. In the middle of the ceiling, a bright blue star shone especially bright.

* * *

Ember took Skylar aside with a glance at Jason. He was busy reading a plaque that described the positions and names of some of the most famous and important galaxies. It would take a while to read.

"We must go to the dungeons," said Ember, turning to Skylar.

"Morgana is not urgent, Ember," said Skylar. "She is locked safely away."

"I need to check on her again," insisted Ember.

"Are you sure? I am not sure whether he is ready. She is an assassin, and a crazy one at that," said Skylar worriedly, glancing at Jason. "Besides, now is not the right time."

"I know," said Ember hurriedly. "But I have been meaning to check on her for some time, and Lu... the Diviner did say that a prisoner would escape."

"It could be any of them, Ember."

"Yes, but Morgana serves Invictius freely. She would do anything in her power to return to him," said Ember.

"I know, but she is unpredictable. If she had a plan, I would expect her to draw less attention to herself."

"As you said, she is unpredictable," said Ember.

Skylar looked at Ember with a thoughtful expression. Ember could see that she was torn between two decisions. It was obvious Jason was not yet ready to encounter Morgana, but Ember could see that Skylar knew she was right; it was time to check on Morgana.

"All right, I suppose it's better to be safe than sorry," said Skylar.

At that moment, Jason turned to them and Skylar and Ember broke apart. Ember glanced at Skylar, who turned away.

"Are these stars and galaxies even in our Realm?" asked Jason, glancing at Skylar as if he knew something was amiss.

"No," replied Ember. "The stars are different in all the Realms, there are a few galaxies they have in common, though."

Jason nodded and turned away.

"Jason," said Skylar hesitantly. "We need to make a quick visit to the dungeons, would you like to come?"

"Okay," said Jason. "I guess."

"Perfect, let's go now. So then we'll be back by lunch," said Ember.

Skylar nodded and touched the door. The glowing words appeared again. She chose one, and Ember readied herself for the dizzying sensation that often came with these types of portals.

They appeared in a long hall. It was much colder than the Star Room. And much, much darker. Ember felt Jason's and Skylar's presence beside her.

CHAPTER FOUR

Ember felt a warmth rush through her, and a sudden light appeared in her hands. She noticed Jason's expression of fear and surprise when he noticed they were flames that enveloped her arms.

"Why are you on fire?" asked Jason, looking faintly confused by her behavior.

"We need light," said Ember. "And we need to get going, come on."

Ember started walking ahead and, after a moment, Skylar and Jason started following.

The underground part of the castle was a maze, with narrow corridors that twisted and turned. Ember took the paths she knew, carefully avoiding the ones that wandered off into nowhere. Before long, she had arrived at a metal gate. Two guards stood in front of it. Their silver staffs glinted in the firelight.

"Who goes there?" called out one of the guards.

"Ember, Status of Huntress, capturer of Morgana, and her two friends, Skylar the Protector and Jason the Keeper."

"The Keeper?" said the other guard. "Do you mean–"

"We are here to see Morgana," interrupted Ember.

"Of course, Ember," said the first guard. "Right this way."

His staff's head transformed into a gleaming silver key. The guard fit the key into the gate's keyhole. With an ominous creaking, the gates opened.

"Follow me," said the guard, leading the way through the gates.

They entered into a corridor even darker than before. Hundreds of cells were on both walls, seemingly going on forever. The gates clanged shut behind them. With a last resounding creak, there was silence. Absolute silence.

Some prisoners were asleep, but most were wide awake. They had dead eyes that stared at Ember with hatred. Some prisoners got up from their beds or where they were sitting to shout insults at Ember. They only had eyes for her. Ember flinched as one particular prisoner started cursing her and throwing stones that had fallen from the ceiling.

"Why are they so mean to Ember?" the whisper reached Ember's ears as Jason asked Skylar.

Skylar sighed. "She put most of them here."

"Oh," said Jason.

The prisoners' words died away as they went deeper underground. The only visible part of the cells in this part of the dungeons was a flat wall of reinforced steel.

"This is where the more dangerous prisoners are kept," whispered Skylar to Jason..

"Behind a wall of metal?" asked Jason, sounding shocked.

Soon the cells disappeared altogether. Before them was a stone wall. The guard touched the stone with his staff, making the wall melt away. The guard ushered Jason and Skylar inside. Ember had already gone on ahead, taking the light with her.

CHAPTER FOUR

They entered a circular room. Jason's breath hung in the air before him. There were thirteen doors, each one of them numbered.

Ember opened the last one. The number thirteen hung from the door in the crude handwriting of a long-dead Wizard. The guard hung back.

"I'll just stay here. Don't stay too long, okay," said the guard, fear apparent in his pale face.

Ember had already slipped inside before he had even finished his sentence. She heard Jason and Skylar quickly follow behind her.

They entered a large, dome-shaped room. Morgana knelt in the middle of the room, her head lowered. Her wrists were shackled to two short chains that were embedded in the floor. Her long, black hair almost touched the ground, and her pointed ears were in plain sight. She wore a drab dress, yet wore it with such elegance that a noble air of royalty hung about her. The sleeves looked charred as though they had been burnt.

The woman looked up as Ember entered. Her eyes were pure black. She smiled condescendingly.

"Hello, dear Ember," said Morgana.

Her gigantic wings opened, revealing burnt feathers that were ink-black. Ember heard Jason gasp.

"Who are your friends?" asked Morgana with a small smile. Her dark eyes glittered in the light of Ember's flames..

"None of your business, Morgana," said Ember.

"Ah. Using first names now, are we?"

Ember looked at her coldly.

"After all this time, you've finally come to visit me. It gets boring, having guards as your only company." Morgana gestured toward the shadows.

Ember didn't have to peer into the shadows to know that there were twenty guards.

"I'm not here to keep you company, Morgana."

"Really?" Morgana pretended to be surprised. "I thought you only came here to chat."

Ember didn't answer.

"Are you here to introduce me to your friends? Or perhaps you're here to let me go?" Morgana's wings spread wider.

"No, Morgana. I'm just here to check on you."

"Oh. That's disappointing," said Morgana, in a mockingly sad voice.

"Yes, it must be," said Ember softly.

"Tell me, Ember. How was your day?"

"It was fine. Onyx attempted to capture the Keeper yesterday, and now we're showing him around."

Morgana smiled maliciously and tutted as if finding a fault in Ember's story.

CHAPTER FOUR

"You let some information slip!" said Morgana in a sing-song voice.

"Well, you're not getting out any time soon. I thought you could use some news."

"Are you getting soft? Or is it that you're afraid that your guest will discover the truth about you?"

Ember's chest tightened. She felt a burning sensation run through her arm. Her hand curled into a fist and the flames burned brighter.

"Of course, we wouldn't want the Keeper to know what you are," continued Morgana, her voice growing bolder. "A princess, a warrior. A fearless hunter, a helpless creature. A Gifted. A traitor."

Ember tightened her fist.

"Don't you dare," said Ember through clenched teeth. "Speak about what I am."

"Of course," said Morgana, bowing her head mockingly. "Your Highness."

"Let's go," said Ember, turning around. "Now."

Jason and Skylar followed her out of the room, the door closing behind them.

Ember walked through the corridor and ignored the prisoner's shouts. She made her staff appear as the second pair of gates started opening. She walked past the guard and only stopped once she had reached the end of the hall.

Jason and Skylar soon caught up with her. And, with a last glance towards the gate, Ember thumped her staff on the ground. Ember, Skylar and Jason disappeared.

CHAPTER FIVE

The Diviner

Xander entered his master's throne room, his long claws scraping the stone floor. Invictius was on his throne, his head bent over a letter he had received, the raven perched on his shoulder.

"Hello, Xander," said Invictius, not looking up from the letter.

"My lord," said Xander, bowing his head.

"You bring news," said Invictius, lifting his head.

"Yes, about the Diviner."

"Do not waste your time telling me," said Invictius, looking at Xander with the faintest gleam of disdain in his deep, black eyes. "Onyx has sent a letter by raven and has told me what she has heard."

"So she has told you that Morgana will escape?"

"No, because that is not what the Diviner has said. All the Diviner said is that a prisoner will escape."

"And it is most likely Morgana."

"Is it our informant that has told you this?" Invictius raised his eyebrows.

"Yes, the double agent."

"You are both foolish. The Diviner did not even mention that the prisoner would be from the castle."

"I–" Xander was cut short.

"I have the Diviner's exact words, here, on this piece of parchment."

"May I see it, my lord?" said Xander, his voice cautious.

"If it will satisfy you," said Invictius.

Invictius waved his hand upward and the letter flew towards Xander. It hung there, immobile. Xander read the letter, his anger growing with every word.

A letter from Onyx, to my master
The Diviners prophecy:

A prisoner of a great kingdom will escape
She will not find her way out alone
Beware, enemy, for years in chains
Have made her long for revenge,
She will have it, therefore bringing your end

Your faithful servant Onyx

As soon as Xander had finished reading it, the letter flew back to Invictius.

CHAPTER FIVE

"Well?" asked Invictius coldly.

"Uh. She? What?" sputtered Xander.

"Yes, that Shadow Wing has to learn some manners, but I have the prophecy now."

"She wrote her name on it!" smoke curled out of Xander's slit-like nostrils.

"I know, but she is telling the truth, and do you not see what it says? It has multiple meanings, therefore we cannot assume that Morgana will escape. It could very well be one of mine."

"But you don't have a kingdom." said Xander, abandoning all cautiousness.

"I do not? Is this not a kingdom? It may be a hidden kingdom but it is a great one."

"Oh, yes of course, my lord," said Xander, regretting his words the moment they left his lips.

"You may leave, Xander," said Invictius, having lost the little patience he possessed. "Come back when you have something useful to say."

Xander bowed his scaly head and made his way out of the door. The doors creaked closed with the echo of impending doom.

* * *

Jason felt the warm sun on his face and slowly opened his eyes. He was blinded for a second when the sunlight hit his pupils. He closed his eyes again and stayed still for a few seconds, enjoying the warmth of the sun on his face.

Jason opened his eyes again and got out of the bed. He jumped when he saw Ember's shadow on the wall. He looked behind him. She was standing in front of the window, staff in hand.

"Good morning," said Ember smilingly.

"Didn't I tell you that's creepy?"

"Y-e-s," said Ember slowly. "But we do need to hurry. Morpheus and Skylar are waiting."

"Oh."

"We'll waste time if you get dressed," said Ember. "Here."

She pointed her staff at his chest. Jason's clothes slowly changed in color and style. It took a few seconds for the transformation to be complete, but once it was finished he was wearing a loose, short-sleeved shirt and baggy cargo pants.

"Let's go then." Ember left through the door.

Jason took a second to put on the sky-blue cloak and ran after her. He caught up with her as they reached the living room doors, which opened as they approached. Skylar was sitting on one of the couches and looked up as they entered. Morpheus was standing up as if he had been watching the doors the whole time.

Ember nodded at Skylar and sat down. Jason sat down opposite Skylar. Morpheus didn't move from where he was standing.

"Jason, we need to leave," said Skylar the second he sat down.

CHAPTER FIVE

"But we just got here," said Jason. He thought Skylar had had something fun in mind, he hadn't been expecting this.

"I know, and I really don't want to go either," said Skylar as Morpheus sniffed doubtfully. "But we really need to leave."

"Why?" asked Jason.

Skylar hesitated and glanced at Morpheus. "Someone spotted Onyx coming to the World of Wizards, and we know she's after you."

"Who's Onyx?"

"A servant of Invictius," said Morpheus. "She's almost as evil as Morgana. You saw how horrid Morgana was and that is because she is a dark creature, a Shadow Wing."

"That is why we need to leave as soon as possible," said Ember.

"You are not coming with us," said Skylar.

"Yes, I am. I want to be there to protect you."

"I am the one that trained you. I taught you everything you know and–"

"Yes, you did teach me everything I know," cut in Ember. "But you also taught me everything you know. That is why it will be safer with me."

"No," said Morpheus with an air of finality. "You are not going, Ember. It will only be me and Skylar that will go with Jason."

"You cannot go!" exclaimed Skylar. "You need to stay with the king."

"He has given me permission to protect the Keeper."

"No," said Jason calmly, surprising even himself at his interruption. "I'm not going until you explain why you call me the Keeper."

There was utter silence as he finished talking. Everyone stared at him in surprise. Skylar looked at Morpheus, who nodded.

"All right, Jason," said Skylar. "If you agree to go, I will tell you."

Jason nodded. He had lost all feeling in his legs.

"There is a Diviner," started Skylar. "She made a prophecy about a boy."

"What did the prophecy say?" asked Jason, feeling a rush of excitement and dread course through his veins.

Skylar looked at Morpheus, who nodded once again.

Skylar flicked her wrist and her staff appeared. The purple orb glowed brighter than Jason had ever seen it, as if it knew something was going to happen. Skylar touched the orb. It flashed for a moment. A screen appeared in the air.

A small girl stood in the middle of the screen, she must have been only four years old. She had bright blue eyes that shone in the semi-dark room she was in.

"I have received a prophecy from the above. It speaks for me, and all these words are true:

CHAPTER FIVE

A boy will come,
Who is Darkness' downfall
The boy has the power of Keeper
The Darkness has the help of a traitor
A world apart, a realm divided
The boy has the power,
The boy is the answer
When Keeper and Darkness last meet
Only one can escape defeat

Understand these words: knowledge is the greatest weapon."

As the girl finished talking the screen flickered and died. Jason felt shivers run down his back.

"This is the reason why we call you the Keeper. We believe you are the boy of which the prophecy speaks," Skylar was saying, but Jason barely heard her.

"Jason?" asked Ember. "Are you okay?"

Jason nodded. He felt numb.

"Jason, this is a lot to take in, I know," said Skylar. "But now you know why we need to leave. Millions of Invictius' followers are after you. They will hurt you."

That woke Jason up.

"Why does it say 'Darkness'?" asked Jason.

"No," said Morpheus. "He is not ready for that information."

Skylar sighed but didn't disagree. Even Ember did not argue.

"Come on! I'm not a kid anymore," Jason said. "I want to know."

"I am sorry, Jason," said Skylar. "But we do not know for sure, and we do not want you to have false hope."

Jason nodded in understanding. Skylar had taken him in when he had lost his parents, though he barely remembered them, and she had loved him and cared for him like a son ever since. He knew she was just trying to protect him.

Silence ensued. An awkward silence that Jason didn't have the strength to break.

"Do you want some breakfast?" asked Skylar, making an attempt at conversation.

"No, I'm good. I'll just go into my bedroom," said Jason. Everything felt so surreal that breakfast felt like a trivial thing.

"I know the way," said Jason. He turned away and walked through the door of the living room. He couldn't see Skylar's face, but thought he could feel her eyes following him.

Jason arrived at his bedroom with a sick feeling in the pit of his stomach. It wasn't from hunger but from a longing that he knew could only be satisfied by finding the person that had made the prophecy.

Jason threw himself on the bed and looked at the ceiling. After only a few seconds he started to become impatient. He got off the bed and started pacing the room. He wanted to leave the room to find the person that had made the prophecy, but Jason knew someone was keeping an eye on him. Skylar was predictable that way.

CHAPTER FIVE

Jason took a last glance around the room to make sure Ember hadn't somehow snuck in. With a last intake of breath, Jason opened the door and left the room. He tiptoed down the stairs. They didn't creak, but at every step he held his breath, sure that someone had seen or heard him.

At the last step Jason sprinted the opposite way, off toward the left. When he turned the corner he slowed down and turned his run into a hasty walk. He looked behind him and gasped as a piercing pain shot through his foot.

"Ow! What did you do that for?" said Jason, as he looked into the assailant's face.

A girl with short, platinum-blonde hair shoved him into the wall, causing Jason's shoulder blades to hit the wall painfully. For a second he was quite sure she meant to kill him.

"Shh," said the girl, the urgency in her voice unmistakable.

"Who are you?" asked Jason, once the girl had let him go.

She glanced around the hall before looking at him again.

"I am Lucinda. I'm sorry I hurt you, I too was sneaking around."

"Why?"

"Ember locked me in my room again. Apparently they showed the Keeper the prophecy and now I'm not even allowed to meet him. I was hoping I would, seeing as we're both Gifted."

"Gifted?"

"Yes, don't you know? The Keeper has all the Gifted powers.

Anyway, what's your name?"

Jason didn't answer. He was thinking over what the girl had just said.

"Hello?" asked Lucinda.

"Oh, yes. My name is Jason."

"Oh. So you're the Keeper? I thought you'd look more impressive." Lucinda was looking him up and down.

"Yeah, um, I'm not supposed to be out of my room…" Jason's words trailed off as he looked at the girl.

"Don't worry, I won't tell anyone. I do it all the time anyway. I know somewhere that we can go where we won't be found anytime soon."

With a final glance around, she walked toward the end of the hall. Jason followed her, but his thoughts were still in turmoil over what she had said.

Lucinda led Jason through a series of corridors. Each emanated the same feeling of being in a magical world. Each was unique in their own way.

They finally arrived in a familiar corridor. Stars that Jason had gotten used to seeing out of his window adorned the ceiling.

"Do you know this place?" asked Lucinda, slipping through the door as it opened. "I heard Ember gave you a tour yesterday."

"Yeah, she did," said Jason, sliding through the door after her.

CHAPTER FIVE

"Was Morpheus with you?" Lucinda looked at him, the bright stars behind her framing her oval-shaped face.

"Yeah."

"He's a bit arrogant, don't you think? He's always arguing with Ember and pointing out her mistakes when he makes plenty of his own."

Lucinda sat down on the floor.

"Yeah, I noticed that," said Jason, sitting down too.

"Anyway they probably said you weren't to go sneaking out of your room otherwise you would meet the Diviner, the one that made the prophecy."

"No, they didn't say anything like that," said Jason, looking up at the starry ceiling.

"Oh, well anyway, I'm the Diviner."

"Really?" said Jason, looking at her in surprise. "I was looking for you. Please, tell me. Do you think it's me?"

"No," said Lucinda truthfully. "I don't. The prophecy says he's a Gifted, otherwise it wouldn't call him 'Keeper', so unless you've shown signs of powers then I doubt it's you."

"Good," said Jason, relief flooding through him.

"You're relieved?" asked Lucinda.

"Yes. All this-" Jason gestured towards the walls of the room.

"Realms, powers, actual bad guys... It's already too much. If I were the one in the prophecy then I don't know what I would do."

"Mm," said Lucinda thoughtfully.

"What?"

"No, nothing. It's just weird that you don't want to be the Keeper. Invictius has killed thousands of people. When the public found out about the prophecy they went crazy. They camped outside the kingdom trying to get an audience with the king. They traveled from all over the Realm just to prove that they were the Destined One."

"Oh," said Jason.

"It's not a bad thing," said Lucinda quickly. "If anything it shows that you don't want glory, or fame. And that's good, it means you are humble."

Jason nodded. Lucinda's words were oddly soothing.

"Anyway, what were you planning to do after you found me?" asked Lucinda.

"Oh, I didn't think of that. My mind was set on looking for you," said Jason, still thinking over what Lucinda had said.

Lucinda smiled. "Are you hungry? I am. I was busy with something today, so I didn't have time for breakfast."

"What were you busy with?"

"I made another prophecy."

CHAPTER FIVE

"Another one? How many do you make?"

"It happens quite often, though it's very annoying. I get splitting headaches whenever it happens."

"Even now?"

"Yes, though my head hurts a bit less because it wasn't a very important prophecy. At least not a the-world-depends-on-this kind of prophecy." Lucinda sighed.

"What was it about?' asked Jason.

Lucinda smiled a bit sadly. "I can't tell you, I'm afraid. Only the Guardians can know."

"The league my aunt works with?"

"Yep," said Lucinda. "That's the one."

Jason nodded, again reminded that Skylar had kept this from him for so many years. Had his mom known? His dad? Was everything in his life a lie?

"Would you like to go get some food?" asked Lucinda again, interrupting Jason's thoughts.

"Sure." They both stood up.

"Where are we going to get food?" asked Jason.

"The kitchen, of course."

Lucinda led the way out of the Star Room and stopped in the middle of the corridor.

"Faster way," explained Lucinda.

Jason nodded, grimacing. Lucinda touched the wall. Glowing words appeared, casting more light on the dim corridor. She chose one of the words and Jason closed his eyes. After a second Jason lost his balance and opened his eyes, discovering that they were in another corridor. He recognized this one too.

"This way," said Lucinda.

She went straight down the corridor, deeper and deeper under the earth. She stopped at a door and knocked. The door creaked open, revealing the cozy and warm interior of the kitchen.

As usual, the sprites were placing the food on the tables and cleaning the floors. Lucinda entered the room and the sprites stopped what they were doing to look at her with expectant faces.

"Excuse me, but could one of you direct me to Willow?"

One of the sprites rushed forward. Lucinda knelt down as it whispered in her ear.

"Thank you," said Lucinda, smiling kindly at the sprite.

As she stood up, the sprites went back to work. They paid no attention to Jason as he passed through.

Lucinda went through the double doors that the sprites came from. The sprites walked around her as she passed them. Jason tried to avoid stepping on the little creatures as he followed her.

The room had a long table in the middle of it. Two large sinks and a huge stove took up the wall ahead of Jason. A dozen fireplaces took up an entire wall. Sprites walked inside the hearths

CHAPTER FIVE

with food and vanished. The room had a pleasant aroma of freshly baked bread and -oddly enough- melting chocolate. There was the soft, comforting clatter of sprites cooking and cleaning.

A few sprites hurried to Lucinda then rushed out of the room, their eyes twinkling merrily. After a few moments they returned, their arms laden with snacks and light foods. Lucinda smiled and picked some sandwiches from the generous feast they laid before her. After exchanging a couple more words with her, the sprites nodded to her and went back to their chores.

Jason slipped between a couple of sprites and moved out of the way as two sprites carried a large pot past him.

"Lucinda!" called Jason.

She didn't seem to hear him, her attention focused on a familiar looking sprite.

"Lucinda!" called Jason again.

Lucinda looked up and smiled as she spotted him amidst the sprites. Jason hurried toward her and narrowly missed a sprite running to the door screaming at the top of its head, telling the other sprites that they had cooked the wrong kind of soup. He pulled out a chair next to Lucinda at the table.

"You got through the crowd all right," said Lucinda as she helped herself to a sandwich.

"Yeah, you know your way around them really well."

Lucinda smiled, a secret twinkling in her eyes as she took a bite out of her sandwich. Jason dug in too.

"Wow, these are awesome," said Jason as he swallowed his mouthful.

"Willow saved them for me. She's kind of in charge of guests, that's how I know her." Lucinda took another bite.

"You're just a guest? I thought you lived here," said Jason.

"I come from the Realm of Sorcerers, but the Head Sorcerers decided it was safer for me to live here. They knew Invictius would be after me when it became public that I had made the prophecy." Lucinda sounded quite cheerful considering a madman was after her.

"I guess they were right, but this place doesn't seem guarded properly."

Lucinda laughed; a sweet, melodic sound that carried through the kitchen.

"There are spells, obviously. Not that you would have known that, seeing how you've been living with Nolmans ever since you were small."

Jason choked on the bread.

"Is that a disease?"

Lucinda laughed again. A few sprites looked up, alarmed.

"Nolman -It's not a disease, it is what we call people with no magical gifts."

"Oh, sorry. I didn't... know."

CHAPTER FIVE

"It's fine," said Lucinda with a small smile.

A sudden, urgent yell came from the next room, and Jason looked up in alarm.

The door imploded, causing the sprites to run into the fireplaces and start to disappear one at a time. Water splashed on the stove and, with a loud hissing, smoke spread throughout the room.

"Where is Jason?" bellowed Ember.

The smoke caused the illusion of a large silhouette. Fires started up in the hearths. The remaining sprites backed away from them in fear.

"If one of you knows where Jason and Lucinda are, then tell me. Trust me, it's the wise thing to do."

Ember became clearer as the smoke cleared away. Her arms were enveloped in flames that naturally would have roasted her flesh. A trembling sprite was pushed forward, away from the crowd. The lone sprite pointed a shuddering finger toward the table, and with a last yelp he disappeared amidst the cloud of sprites.

Ember looked toward the table, the flames on her arms dying down once she spotted Jason and Lucinda. The sleeves of Ember's cloak were incinerated up to the shoulders, but she didn't seem to notice this as she ran to Lucinda and hugged her tightly. She let go almost immediately and looked at Jason. He smiled shyly, not sure what mood Ember was in.

"How could you just vanish like that?" asked Ember sharply.

"Sorry," said Jason, avoiding her gaze.

"Skylar was worried, and I thought you had been kidnapped. I searched everywhere. I got angry at Morpheus and threw a fireball at him. He has a burn on his chest now, but he's fine…" Ember rattled on until her voice dwindled as she ran out of breath.

"You can't do that," said Ember, her voice low. "We're risking our necks trying to keep you alive, and safe. The Guardians are against Invictius, but they side with Morpheus regarding you; so if you go running off, Skylar and I get in trouble." Ember looked at Jason with dread in her eyes.

"I'm sorry," mumbled Jason.

He realized how foolish he had been to sneak off. Lucinda had meant the best, but perhaps he should have returned to his room.

"It's fine now, I found you and you're okay. Let's just go," said Ember.

"Can I stay here?" asked Lucinda.

Ember's eyes flashed scarlet. "No. It's already bad enough you two met; I'll bring Jason back to his room, you will go with Willow," said Ember.

Willow came running toward them.

"I am here, mistress! Come, Lucinda, we must go."

Lucinda winked at Jason merrily, though the guilt was plain in her eyes. Ember watched Lucinda go then turned to Jason. She looked tired and impatient.

"Come on, Jason," sighed Ember, walking out of the room.

CHAPTER FIVE

Jason took a last glance around the kitchen. The fires in the hearths had died down to small flames. The sprites were cleaning up the mess on the stove and the scorch marks on the door. Jason sighed and followed Ember, though his thoughts were still on Lucinda and what she had said.

the Keeper of the Elements

CHAPTER SIX

Lady Lavinia

Morpheus seated himself at the head of the table. All the Guardians were there. Skylar was on his right and Ember was on his left. Both of them were watching him. All the Guardians had their eyes on him.

"As you all know, the Destined One is here in the castle," said Morpheus.

A few heads nodded, others just sniffed reprovingly.

"Skylar may be convinced that he is the One, but I am sure that the prophecy would not speak about him. We all know how the father turned out," said one of the Guardians.

She had dark, beady eyes and a curly head of ginger hair. Her stern mouth was set in a thin line.

"Yes, Lady Dracnel, thank you for your insight," said Morpheus quickly. "We do know how the father turned out, but at least this time we can stop it from happening to the son. He is destined to destroy Darkness, so I am quite sure that he will not turn to the dark side in the first place."

More Guardians nodded and gave Lady Dracnel heated looks.

"However, we are not here for that, we are here to discuss the sightings of Onyx," continued Morpheus, looking at each Guardian in turn.

"Yes," said Skylar. "We are. Morpheus and I called this meeting to discuss whether we should move to the mountains and take refuge in the Sacred Temples of the Ancient."

A few Guardians gasped in surprise and shock, while Ember just looked on silently.

"Move there? As you said, Skylar, it is a sacred and ancient place. No-one is allowed there but the worthy," Lady Dracnel spoke again.

"Lady Dracnel," said Cliff Souls, an old knight. "How is anyone supposed to enjoy these meetings with you yammering on and on and on?"

Sir Souls had wispy, graying hair covering one of his eyes. He smiled, showing missing teeth. Some Guardians laughed and looked fondly at him. Morpheus allowed himself a small smile, though Cliff sometimes irritated him with his nonchalant attitude.

"Thank you, Sir Souls, but please do not start an argument," said Morpheus. Sir Souls nodded and lifted his hands placatingly.

"Now," continued Morpheus as if there had never been any interruption, "who votes that we go there to take refuge and train the boy in his powers?" asked Morpheus.

"Excuse me, Morpheus," said a Guardian.

The Guardians peered toward the foot of the table, where the one who had spoken was seated. She had long, pearl-colored hair that flowed over her fur shawl. Her eyes were a shocking green that could warm the heart of the coldest mountain creature, yet at the same time chill you to your core.

"Yes, Duchess Luna Lavinia?" asked Morpheus.

Duchess Lavinia stood up elegantly, the fur shawl draped around her neck a firm reminder of her noble blood.

"The prophecy says that the boy is the Keeper, which we all know to mean he holds the Elements and controls them as he controls his actions and movements," said the Duchess, pausing for effect.

There was absolute silence. Only a scattered few nodded.

"Why do we not test him?" said the Duchess, lifting one delicate shoulder questioningly.

The Guardians gasped at her words. Even Skylar could not hold back an exclamation of horror.

"If he truly is the One then he will not suffer or be hurt–" continued the Duchess

"—and if he isn't then he will die!" said Skylar.

At this, yells broke out.

"Kill an innocent child?"

"How could you!?"

"He is a small boy, you would kill him!"

"Quiet!" said Morpheus, the word reverberating through the room.

Silence fell upon the Guardians as they looked at Morpheus. Duchess Lavinia glanced at Skylar and sat down, but did not utter another word. Ember glanced at the Duchess with a look of disgust. Lady Dracnel looked oddly pale and glanced at the Duchess. Sir Souls was the only one who did not look perturbed in the least.

"We are not here to see if he is truly the Destined One," said Morpheus, his voice penetrating the now-silent room. "I called this meeting to vote if we should go to the Sacred Temples of the Ancient. If you want we can also vote to test the boy, but the real question is if we should go or not."

"Let us vote then," said Sir Souls.

"Thank you, Cliff," said Morpheus, inclining his head toward him.

"Who votes for us to go?" asked Skylar.

Morpheus, Ember and Skylar raised their hands, as did Cliff Souls and a few other Guardians.

"Who votes against?"

The Duchess and Lady Dracnel raised their hands, only two others agreeing with them.

"The majority wins! We are going," said Skylar, a small smile of relief passing over her face.

"Wait a moment," said Duchess Lavinia.

CHAPTER SIX

Morpheus glared at her.

"Who is going with him?" Duchess Lavinia looked around the room, the other Guardians looking as confused as her.

"Me, Ember and Skylar are going with the boy," said Morpheus.

"And did we agree to this?" asked Duchess Lavinia.

"There is no need for a vote, but since I am his guardian then I will obviously go. I cannot speak for Morpheus or Ember though," said Skylar.

"I am going because I have studied the dark creatures we will meet, such as Shadow Wings and Dark Wolves," said Morpheus.

"And you, Ember? What is your reason?" said the Duchess, turning to Ember.

"I have experience with forests. You all remember the time Morpheus accused me and I went into hiding," said Ember, a hint of distaste in her eyes at the memory. "I hid in various forests scattered across the Realm, all were dangerous and not at all fun."

"I suppose all of you have your reasons, that is true. But what if I were to come?" asked the Duchess.

"You are accustomed to a life of luxury. I do not think you would enjoy the journey," said Skylar.

"Well, an extra guardian for the boy can't hurt."

"All right, I suppose it would be all right for you to join us. We are leaving today, after lunch," said Morpheus.

"Expect me at the front door," said Duchess Lavinia, smiling as she stood to leave.

* * *

"Jason?" asked Ember, opening the door.

Jason was putting on his dragonhide cloak, the black scales glinting in the sunlight.

"Yeah?" said Jason, slipping his arms through the sleeves.

"We need to go. Morpheus and Skylar are waiting."

"Okay."

Jason grabbed a pack that was on his bed and followed Ember out the door. She led him down the stairs and through a few halls. They finally arrived at the front door where Skylar and Morpheus were waiting for them. A lady that Jason didn't recognize was sitting down on a plush one-seater couch. She sat up as Ember and Jason approached and the couch disappeared.

"You got everything?" Skylar asked Jason.

"Yes," said Jason, glancing at the lady.

"Jason, this is Duchess Luna Lavinia, she will be accompanying us on the journey," said Morpheus, gesturing toward the lady.

"Hello," said Jason.

The Duchess nodded in his direction.

CHAPTER SIX

"It will take a few weeks to get there," said Skylar, keeping her eyes away from the Duchess.

"Why can't we just transport there?" asked Jason.

"Because the Temples and the land surrounding it have anti-transporting spells," said Ember.

"Oh, okay."

"Let us get going then, we have a long journey ahead of us," said the Duchess.

Skylar nodded and flicked her wrist. Her staff appeared in her hand, the orb glowing brightly.

"Shall I do the honors?"

"Go ahead," said the Duchess curtly.

Skylar took a second to glare at her, then concentrated on her staff. The purple engravings shone brighter and –in a flash of violet light– the group disappeared.

Jason gasped as he fell face first into a mound of snow. He heard a thud behind him and the crunch of snow. Someone helped him up; the hand felt really warm. He looked up into Ember's face. She glanced at the Duchess, who was standing beside a tree covered in icicles. Ember walked over to Skylar and helped her up as Skylar's staff disappeared.

"Where are we?" asked Jason, spitting out snow.

"In the Forest of Time," answered Skylar.

"Time is not normal here," said Ember. "That's where it gets its name obviously. A Wizard once cast a spell at the same time as a time Gifted, or Time Holder, as they are often called, and the spells became intertwined…"

"Cool!" Jason blurted out.

"It is not the best place to be," said Skylar. "Because time can go slow or fast here, so today it may seem like winter but before you know it, it will be spring. Or it will be winter for most of the year."

"Can we wrap this up?" asked the Duchess, her thin brows raised questioningly.

"Yes of course, your majesty," said Skylar drily.

"No arguing please," said Morpheus. "We need to get moving, come along."

Ember followed Morpheus and the Duchess followed her. Skylar steered Jason behind the Duchess and brought up the rear.

The party walked through the forest in silence, the only sound the crunching of the snow. Suddenly the screams of a flock of birds exploded over their heads, the noise dwindling as the birds flew south.

Jason looked around and found himself appreciating the beauty of the forest. The trees were covered in snow and their branches drooped elegantly under the weight of it. The ground was covered in pearly white snow, and if it wasn't for the bright colors of Morpheus' staff, Jason would have imagined he had ended up in a black and white photograph.

CHAPTER SIX

The group walked all afternoon, resting only when necessary and drinking the water that Skylar had brought.

Dusk fell in slow motion, the sun taking a full ten minutes to set. The moon was covered by the overshadowing clouds and there was almost no light left to see by. The stars came out one by one and shone brighter than any stars Jason had ever seen.

"All right, time to set up camp for tonight," said Ember, once they had reached a clearing.

Morpheus nodded. The Duchess sat down on a large, flat rock.

"Come on," said Ember, who seemed to be enjoying ordering Morpheus about.

Ember told Morpheus and the Duchess to start making the clearing more suitable to sleep in. The Duchess conjured four tents, and Morpheus started casting spells all around.

Skylar had summoned a feast in a matter of seconds, and the Duchess summoned more than a couple pillows to lean against.

"All right," said Ember, her arms laden with kindling and logs. "I got the wood, now time for a fire."

"You're the expert on that," said Skylar.

Ember smiled and dumped the wood at the edge of the clearing. She organized it into a pyramid. When she had finished she reached into the heart of the pile. Jason saw a flicker of fire, and in a second the whole pile was burning merrily. Ember slowly withdrew her hand from the flames. She was so close to them that Jason was amazed she didn't catch fire.

"How does she do that?" whispered Jason to Skylar.

"She's a Gifted," answered Skylar simply.

"A Gifted? I heard about them from Lucinda, but she hadn't said anything about Ember."

"She doesn't like to display it," said Skylar softly.

She looked at Jason and seemed to notice the anxiety written across his face.

"Is something wrong?" asked Skylar.

"If I am the Keeper, then what does that mean? Who am I supposed to be?" burst out Jason.

Skylar sighed and avoided meeting his eyes.

"Well, Keepers can be any creature in the Seven Realms," said Skylar. "But they are so hard to find and keep in one place that no-one's ever properly studied them."

Someone coughed politely. Jason looked up. The Duchess was waiting expectantly next to the feast Skylar had prepared.

"Yes?" asked Skylar, doing her best to be civil.

"When are we going to dine? I am starved," said the Duchess, her tone implying that she thought it was quite obvious what she wanted.

"Then eat, the food isn't going anywhere," said Skylar.

CHAPTER SIX

"Enough, you two. You are both mature adults, the least I expect from you is to act like it," said Morpheus.

Ember turned to look at him with an accusing glare.

"Now," said Morpheus. "Is dinner ready?"

"Yes," said Skylar.

She and Jason sat around the flat rock that functioned as their makeshift dining table. Morpheus sat down on a nearby rock. His golden staff disappeared as he reached for a plate.

"Ember, come away from the fire and stop making shapes in it," said Skylar in a motherly tone.

Jason looked away from Ember and sat down next to Skylar on the soft blanket. Ember turned away from the roaring fire and sat across from Jason.

Their first meal together was a silently tense affair. Once they had finished, Skylar and Ember cleaned up with the reluctant help of the Duchess.

"Here is your blanket, Jason," said Skylar, handing him a blanket as he slid into his sleeping bag. "Goodnight."

She closed the tent and Jason watched her blurred silhouette as she walked to the fire. It took only a couple of moments for him to fall asleep.

* * *

Skylar joined the others around the fires. Ember was on a log next to her, the flames reflecting in her eyes. Morpheus had made his staff appear and was polishing it. The Duchess had wrapped a blanket around herself and was sitting close to the fire, her furs on display as usual.

Ember was creating the shapes and silhouettes of animals and people within the flames, but stopped at a sign from Skylar.

"I think he is asleep," said Skylar, with a backward glance at Jason's tent.

"What is your plan?" asked the Duchess. For once, her voice was not harsh.

"I was thinking of teaching him about the elements. The journey seemed the best time to do so. We could take pauses on some days and try to teach him," replied Skylar.

"I don't know," said Ember, subconsciously making a dragon within the flames. "He can barely grasp that Realms exist. I fear that it will be too much."

"I think talking to Lucinda helped him," said Skylar. "He doesn't seem as shaken or distracted as when we first came here."

"Yes, I agree," said Morpheus. "He seems to have accepted that he is the Keeper."

"I think we made the right decision showing him the prophecy. He seems at ease now," said Skylar softly.

The Duchess nodded her head.

"I have had my fair share of new Wizards or Sorcerers, and he seems to accept the concept of magic much better than many of the others."

CHAPTER SIX

"I just hope he will be okay after we teach him his gifts," said Skylar.

"I am sure he will," said Morpheus reassuringly

"Lucinda will meet us there I presume?" asked Ember, looking up at Skylar.

"No, her destination changed at the last minute," said Skylar.

"Lucinda? What destination?" asked the Duchess incredulously. "We did not speak of this in any of the Guardian meetings! Lucinda is in our care. All the Guardians must protect her! You are saying that she would have met us there, and you hadn't even consulted the rest of the Guardians."

"Keep your voice down," said Skylar sharply. "We did not tell you because we knew the Guardians would disagree. And we hid it from you also because we suspect there is a traitor in our midst."

"A traitor?" said the Duchess. "A traitor in the castle?"

"A traitor or a spy, we do not know which. But we must take all the precautions necessary," said Morpheus.

"And you trust me with this?" asked the Duchess, looking from Morpheus to Skylar.

"Yes," said Morpheus. "You have been my dear friend for many years and a great help after the Third World War."

The Duchess nodded.

"I know that you trust me," said the Duchess, her eyes still on Skylar. "But does Skylar?"

Skylar hesitated; the past was past. But she still couldn't forget the memory that was planted in her mind.

"I used to trust you. You are in the Legion of the Guardians, therefore part of my team. I should not be against you but should work with you."

"I know. But do you trust me?"

"No," said Skylar simply. "How could I trust someone who betrayed me? I used to trust you with my life, but then you went against me. You helped Invictius kill Amethyst. I could never forgive the person who killed Jason's mother."

The Duchess nodded, her face bereft of any expression that might reveal her emotions.

"I understand," said the Duchess after a long silence. "Does the boy know where we are going?"

"Please do not call him "the boy"," said Skylar coldly. "His name is Jason. But no, he does not know. If he asked, I would tell him. But I do not see why I should tell him more than is needed."

"So you are keeping the truth from him?" asked the Duchess bluntly.

Skylar looked away. "He is my nephew. I am just trying to protect him."

"Of course," said the Duchess coldly

"We should go to sleep," said Skylar suddenly.

CHAPTER SIX

The Duchess nodded and stood up, soon disappearing in her tent. Skylar sighed and glanced at Ember, she bid Morpheus goodnight and went to her own tent, welcoming a sleepless night.

the Keeper of the Elements

CHAPTER SEVEN

Plans

Onyx moved forward quietly and balanced herself on the thick branch with her wings. She lowered herself to the ground, flapping her wings, so that she did not hit the ground too quickly. She landed on the ground with a soft crunch, crushing the fallen leaves with her bare feet.

"Onyx."

A deep, menacing voice came from behind the shadows of the trees. It was not human and spoke in a growl.

"Yes, Alpha?" said Onyx, turning to face the creature that came out of the shadows.

A giant wolf stepped out in front of her. He had glossy, ink-black fur. His eyes were an evil green that shone in the semi-dark forest. He growled softly, revealing numerous deadly teeth.

"Do you have news?" asked Onyx casually.

"Yes, the impostor heard that the Keeper is going to the Sacred Temples of the Ancient."

"Not by himself, surely."

"He is being accompanied by four other people. Three of them are fully grown. The fourth, a girl, is barely older than the boy. But I warn you to be careful of her. She is the capturer of Morgana the Murderer, and she has captured many of Invictius' followers."

"Mm," said Onyx thoughtfully. "I will have to deal with her in a special way. What of the other three?"

"The king's advisor is guiding the boy, as well as the Duchess of the East and the boy's aunt."

"The Duchess of the East? I thought she was a creature of luxury," said Onyx in a disbelieving tone.

"Yes, it is very odd," said the Alpha in a bored tone.

"Ah, you are angry that Invictius will not send you on a worthwhile mission. Well, you can't always have what you want," said Onyx with a smile.

"Why are we here? Can we not capture the boy before he leaves?" said the Alpha, obviously itching for some excitement and —possibly— death.

"He has already left. I searched his room; there were no clothes and the bed was made."

"How did you enter the boundary that surrounds the castle?"

"The magical border? That was a trivial thing, all I had to do was steal a guard's staff. They always have something hidden in the orb, usually a key."

The Alpha grunted in annoyance, but the flutter of wings caught Onyx's attention.

CHAPTER SEVEN

"Finally," sighed Onyx fondly. "Here it is."

A raven came flying toward her. In its claws it held a long bag made of dragon-hide.

"What is it?" asked the Alpha.

"My bow," said Onyx as she grabbed the bag from the bird.

The raven struggled for a moment, trying to free its claw. With a last effort it broke free and flew over the trees, disappearing from Onyx's sight. Onyx opened the bag tenderly, uncovering her companion on all her missions.

A beautiful, finely carved wooden bow came into sight. Intricate, silver engravings adorned the curved wood. The string that connected both ends was made of unicorn hair collected by Onyx herself. The arrows were the finest in the Realms: they were made of Wish Wood, giving them the ability to grant the holder any desire. The quiver was made of dragon hide, which was fire-proof, impervious to magic, and would keep anything inside it preserved and unaged.

"How I missed you," said Onyx, stroking the wood of her bow.

"Of course it is your bow. What else could it be," said the Alpha.

"Do not ruin the moment, Alpha," said Onyx, turning to him threateningly.

The Alpha stiffened but backed away. Onyx turned back to her bow and gently lifted the quiver. She shouldered it and smiled.

"Time to go hunting."

* * *

"Jason. Jason!"

Jason was shaken awake. His eyes snapped open and looked straight into the hazel eyes of Ember.

"Finally," said Ember. "You sleep really deeply, by the way."

Jason couldn't help but smile at her comment as he turned to slip out from under the covers. He followed her out of his tent and shivered in the winter air. Jason glanced at Skylar, who was already packing away the dishes.

"Am I too late?" asked Jason as he approached her.

"No, I salvaged some bread for you. But you'll have to eat it while we're walking." She handed him a small loaf of bread.

Jason nodded understandingly.

"Finally awake, are we?" said the Duchess, smiling at Jason.

"Good morning," said Jason nervously. This was the first time the Duchess had spoken to him since they had met.

"Ah, we were waiting for you," said Morpheus. "We can be on our way now that you're awake."

Jason nodded nervously, Morpheus was so tall Jason had to crane his neck a bit. For a moment Jason wondered if Morpheus' towering height was due to a spell. Ember came up behind Jason. He started as her sleeve brushed his shoulder.

"Time to go," said Ember.

CHAPTER SEVEN

The Duchess swept her staff over the blankets and they disappeared. Morpheus started walking northward, slowly allowing them to catch up. Skylar handed Jason his dragon scale cloak.

"Put it on," said Skylar, as the Duchess walked past them and followed Morpheus.

Jason slipped the cloak on and started eating his breakfast as they walked northward, toward the Temples.

Progress was slow, the ground starting to get rockier as they walked more up-hill. The trees did not help. Morpheus, in the lead, would slow down every once in a while and magically hack off a branch or two, making the path easier for everyone else. Jason noticed some branches Morpheus cut off would grow back in mere seconds. It was a majestic and beautiful cycle that made Jason stop to watch it be completed.

"Keep on walking, Jason," said Skylar, when he stopped to see a winter flower grow back along with its branch.

"Sorry," said Jason as he continued walking.

The sun slowly reached the top of the sky; it did not help with the cold, but it was reassuring to know that they would stop soon. Jason took a last, desperate step to the top of the hill. He collapsed from exhaustion onto the icy snow.

"Jason? Are you alright?" asked Skylar worriedly, hurrying to his side.

"Yeah, just really tired," said Jason, turning to face her.

"Ember, make a fire," said Skylar.

Jason heard the crunch of snow as Ember turned away, undoubtedly to collect some wood. Skylar helped Jason sit up and fixed the cloak around his neck. Jason looked up as Ember came back with the wood. It was not very much, but Jason was positive she could manage even without it. He was reminded of when she had stormed inside the kitchen and fires had erupted in the hearths.

At Ember's command, a crackling fire started burning merrily. The warmth brought back some feeling in Jason's numb and cold fingers.

"That feels better," said the Duchess. "Thank you, Ember."

Ember nodded and turned back to the fire, which grew in height when she held out her hand. Morpheus moved closer to the fire, moving as close as he could without getting singed.

"Who wants sandwiches?" asked Skylar, summoning her staff.

"I would love some," said the Duchess.

Jason glanced at Morpheus just in time to see him look away.

"What?" asked Jason.

"Nothing, nothing."

Nothing more was said, but Jason couldn't help but feel that there was something Morpheus was hiding.

"Skylar," said Jason, as a sudden thought came to his mind.

"Yes, dear?"

"Where are we going?"

Skylar looked away from him. Morpheus too, looked oddly uncomfortable, but attempted to hide it by looking away. The Duchess turned away from the conversation and stared into the fire. Ember was the only one that looked Jason square in the face.

"You said you would tell him if he asked," said the Duchess, not looking up from the flames.

Skylar hesitated. Ember and Morpheus watched them silently.

"Skylar, please tell me. I want to know," said Jason.

"I suppose now is as good a time as any," sighed Skylar, turning to Jason with a faint smile on her lips. "We are going to an ancient place, built by the very first Gifted. It is a place between Realms, a safe haven. This place is called the Sacred Temples of the Ancient. It is a place of healing, restoration and learning. Though it has been abandoned for a millennium it still has the protection placed there by the founders."

"The founders?" asked Jason, finding himself being drawn in by Skylar's words.

"The nine founders, also the first Gifted, were already thousands of years old. They built the Temples as a place to keep their memories, so that whoever came through their haven would acquire knowledge and wisdom." Skylar gazed into the fire's center, the flames reflected in her eyes. "It is a beautiful place. Golden trees decorate the gardens and the Nine Temples are made of Evallinium, the most valuable metal in all the Realms. Fairies brush across your face and glow brighter than fireflies once the sun sets. The Great Lake shimmers like ice, and merpeople will sometimes come to the surface to welcome newcomers. It is the most wonderful place anyone can ever go."

"It sounds amazing," whispered Jason in awe.

"It is. I cannot wait to see it again."

Jason suddenly felt much better. The way Skylar had described the Temples made it sound like a fairy tale.

"Who would like to eat?" asked Skylar, after a blissful silence.

Skylar handed each of the weary travelers a couple of sandwiches, which they dug into cheerfully.

"Thank you, Skylar," said Jason, taking the first bite out of his sandwich.

Skylar nodded and sat down to eat her own sandwiches. For a while the only sound was the chewing of bread. Ember abruptly stopped eating and watched Jason for a while. Soon the rest of the group had noticed her intent staring. Jason was the only one oblivious to her gaze and finished the sandwiches with relish. He looked up as he swallowed the last bite and was startled to find everyone looking at him and Ember.

"Is something wrong?" asked Jason hesitantly.

"When will you tell him?" Ember asked Skylar, though her gaze did not move from the confused Jason.

"I did not think now was the right time, Ember."

"You said you would tell him!" said Ember.

She stood up, her sleeve accidentally brushing the fire and starting to burn. Ember shook her arm and the flames disappeared.

CHAPTER SEVEN

"Come on, tell him what you are going to teach him," said Ember, her eyes glittering with anger.

"Alright, Ember. I will tell him," said Skylar.

Ember nodded, suddenly calm, and sat back down. The only sign of impatience was her hand making vivid images in the fire.

"What are you talking about? What are you going to teach me?" asked Jason, turning to Skylar.

"I was wondering when the right time would be to tell you about the lessons we will be having." Skylar paused, as if to see Jason's reaction.

"Lessons? Of what?" asked Jason, more curious than he would have been if Ember hadn't said anything.

"Lessons of your powers. Usually each Gifted only has one power of the Gifts. The Keeper of the Elements is the only one who has all the Gifts."

"What?" said Jason, speechless with surprise.

Skylar smiled. The Duchess and Morpheus shifted uneasily but they both had a kindly twinkle in their eyes. Even Ember didn't look angry anymore.

"You can't be serious. I'm pretty sure I don't have any powers, I haven't ever done anything out of the ordinary."

"I know, Jason, but we are quite sure. The prophecy speaks of a boy. Invictius is after you and if you pass a test we give you we'll be sure you're the Destined One."

"A test?" asked the Duchess, interrupting their conversation. "You said that we would not test him."

"Morpheus and I found an unharmful way," answered Skylar quite calmly.

"Really? And it is foolproof?"

"Yes," said Skylar.

"All right," said the Duchess. "But may I know in what way you are going to test him?"

"We are going to use Lavaneim."

The Duchess gasped. "Lavaneim?"

"Yes."

"Where did you acquire it?" asked the Duchess.

"The elves generously gave a small portion of it to me."

"Excuse me," said Ember quickly. "But don't you think we should explain to Jason what 'Lavaneim' is?"

"Oh, of course," said Skylar, turning to Jason with a smile.

"Lavaneim is a type of metal that is also called the Metal of the Gifted. It is called this because it reveals a Gifted's powers, but it is also very dangerous because it makes the Gifted's powers uncontrollable. I want to use this way of revealing whether you are the Keeper, because the way the Duchess suggested would most likely be fatal."

"What did she suggest?" asked Jason, fearing her answer.

"She wanted to put you in a physical body of a Gifted power, for example fire or water. If you were not the Gifted though, or if you had no idea of how to control it… well, then you would die."

"Oh," said Jason, surprised by the cruelty of the Duchess.

"I am sorry," said the Duchess. "I was… insensitive."

"Yes, you were," said Skylar coldly.

"Shouldn't we get going?" asked Morpheus.

"Oh. But I was wondering if we would have time to teach Jason a bit," said Skylar.

"Alright, but let's use a Vortex spell," said Morpheus.

"The Hidden Universe spell?" asked Ember excitedly.

"Yes, it is the most effective way of hiding if Onyx knows where we are or if she's seen us."

"Yes!" said Ember, her smile widening. "Can I do it?"

"I suppose. Do you know the incantation?"

"Yes."

"Uh, what is a 'Vortex Spell'?" asked Jason.

"A person called Vortex found a way to create some spells," said Ember, ready with an answer. "One of these spells is a Hidden Spell, it creates a room — at least that is what Wizards call it.

The room you create is a place where you can go without fear of being seen or heard by the people of any Realm."

"Sounds confusing."

"It is," said Ember happily.

"All right Ember, on my mark," said Skylar, as she finished gathering the last of the things.

"Right," said Ember, quickly summoning her staff.

Ember closed her eyes, the scarlet orb shining blood-red light on the snow. A swirling hole of red and black started expanding above Ember, and the wind rushed through the trees.

A flash of blinding red light appeared, then silence and absolute darkness. Jason slowly opened his eyes. He stood in a field of swaying grass and bright flowers. An explosion of sound behind him, a flock of birds, thundered away in the sky.

"What is this place?" Jason's voice echoed through the Universe.

"Ember, where did you take us?" asked Morpheus, his voice clearer than Jason's.

"Hidden Universe," answered Ember, her hand shaking.

"You imagined the room being like this?" asked the Duchess. Her voice did not echo, and the sounds around Jason started to become more distinct.

"Yes," said Ember. Her eyes flashed scarlet.

CHAPTER SEVEN

"It is all right Ember, you do not need to say anything," said Skylar, glaring at Morpheus and the Duchess.

"Where is the Lavaneim?" asked the Duchess.

"Right here," said Skylar, gesturing to one of the packs she had taken from the camp. "Jason, kneel down on the ground and close your eyes."

Jason did as she said, though all his instincts told him to run away. He closed his eyes and felt a shiver run through him. Fear grasped him from his heart. He felt himself freeze, as if his body -his mind- knew the Lavaneim had been uncovered.

"Open your eyes, Jason," said Skylar.

Jason opened his eyes and looked at the surface of a shining metal orb. He felt himself tense. Something exploded behind him, and a long, threatening root curled up in the air.

A loud blast of wind rushed through the field, whipping Jason's hair into his eyes and making his cloak rise in the air. The wind howled ferociously as if it was mourning.

Drops of water were drawn out of the ground and surrounded Jason. The water hid him behind a curtain of floating droplets, suspended in the air.

Flickering flames surrounded Jason in a ring. The fire avoided the water and rose to towering heights, but Jason didn't feel the heat.

The water froze in slow motion. Ice curled around Jason in the shape of a spiral.

Thunder roared over Jason. Lightning struck just inches from him.

Jason felt his eyes roll back in his head. He couldn't hear Skylar shouting as he leaned forward. His hands felt alive with energy.

A trembling cloak of Jason's own shadow stretched across the ground. Long, spidery fingers brushed against the ring of fire in its urgency to escape. Shadow emerged from the darkness.

Hundreds of voices echoed inside Jason's head: screaming, sad voices. And others that were happy and joyous. Jason screamed from the pain, clutching his head with trembling hands.

Time slowed down and the voices died down. Slowly, majestically, a lightning bolt struck the ground. The sky lit up for a second before the light disappeared again. Time stopped entirely. A lightning bolt paused between the ground and the dark, rolling clouds in the sky.

Jason suddenly felt calm. The silence was absolute, the void endless.

The enchantment broke, and time returned to normal. Skylar stuffed the Lavaneim orb back into the pack. The Earth retreated back to where it came from. The air stood still again. Water splashed onto the ground as the ice surrounding it cracked and melted. The fire died away in an instant, leaving behind it a scorched, black line. The sky grew clear and the lightning struck no more. Jason's shadow crept back to its rightful place, and Jason felt a tingling sensation as his soul settled back down.

"Are you all right, Jason?" asked Skylar. He barely heard her. Her gentle voice was dim, and it echoed distantly.

CHAPTER SEVEN

"Jason?" Now Ember was calling. She took hold of his shoulder and shook him until his eyes snapped open. Everything looked fuzzy and distorted. Jason groaned and felt his head. He couldn't hear the voices anymore, and hoped they were gone for good, but the pain was as sharp as ever.

"Is he all right?" Jason could barely discern the voice of the Duchess.

"Yes, of course he is," said Morpheus, sounding worried.

"What happened?" said Jason, his eyes focusing on Skylar's anxious face.

"It's all my fault. I should have never done this. It almost killed you."

"That is not true," said Ember, putting her arm around Skylar.

"We did not know what it would do, Skylar. It is my fault as much as yours," said Morpheus. His tone was dignified but Jason could see that he was struggling to keep it that way.

"At least now we know he has powers," said the Duchess.

"I suppose," said Skylar. "But the important thing is that he is alive."

"Of course," said the Duchess.

"Jason, do you feel well enough to start the lesson?" said Skylar.

Jason nodded. He couldn't say anything: simply opening his mouth took strength he didn't have.

"Let's give him some Pure Water," said Morpheus, opening his pack and taking out an old, worn-out flask.

"Good idea," said Skylar, accepting the flask he offered her.

"What will it do?" asked Jason, wincing as he stretched his jaw to speak.

"It will give you strength," said Skylar, taking off the top of the flask.

Jason gulped down as much as he could –which was all of it– and smiled at Skylar as he handed back the empty flask.

"Thanks," said Jason, sighing in relief.

Skylar's eyes twinkled kindly as she smiled back. The Duchess was looking away from them, seemingly lost in her own thoughts. Morpheus put the flask back in its proper place and stood up. Ember, too, stood up.

"Where are you going?" asked Skylar when she noticed this.

"I thought it would be better if Jason was only with you," said Morpheus, glancing at the Duchess, who stood up too.

"Oh, well it's all right for you two to leave," said Skylar, gesturing to Morpheus and the Duchess. "But I thought it would be helpful if Ember stayed and helped, seeing as she has a Gifted power too."

"Actually, I wasn't going to leave," said Ember. "I wanted to go for a walk."

CHAPTER SEVEN

"Oh, well then go for a few minutes and enjoy yourself, the first lessons are quite boring anyway," said Skylar.

Ember nodded and — with a sweep of her blood-red cloak — was gone.

"All right then. Goodbye," said Morpheus. He nodded to the Duchess and his staff materialized. The next second they were both gone.

"All right Jason," said Skylar, smiling with relief at the silence the field was now immersed in. "We will start with the gift of earth."

"The first thing you need to learn about earth is that it is solid. It is the most solid of the original elements, which are earth, water, air and fire. Water can bend and take up the shape of its container. Air is a gas and can be powerful when you want it to, but for the most part it gives life. Fire is a mysterious element, but also the most dangerous. It should only be used when you need something unpredictable and when you know you have absolute control over it."

Jason hesitantly raised his hand. He wasn't sure how to demonstrate that he wanted to ask a question.

"Yes, Jason?" asked Skylar, her voice sterner than usual, but Jason could still detect the gentle and kind tone he had learned to answer to his whole life.

"What exactly are Shadow Wings?"

"Oh, of course. Onyx, the one trying to kill you, is a Shadow Wing. They are the most dangerous creatures you will ever meet, and most of them have rallied against Wizards and Sorcerers and are fighting for Invictius."

"What do they look like?" asked Jason curiously.

"They are described as fearsome beasts. They have wings twice the size of their body and have sharp features. Though they do not have powers they are usually very accomplished with weapons and destroy anything in their path once they have their heart set on it."

"So they're dangerous?"

"Yes. Very dangerous."

"Do they have a weakness?" asked Jason.

"Arrogance is perhaps their only weakness. Though they have gone into hiding, they only went because they are Dark Creatures and hate every living thing. I would not advise you to go looking for them, because they would most likely kill you."

"Oh," said Jason. He hadn't been thinking of looking for them. He was just curious.

"All right, the first thing you need to do is clear your mind. Earth is all around you, and there is so much of it that if you do not clear your mind then you cannot control it."

"How do I clear my mind?" asked Jason, simultaneously trying to make his mind blank.

"You must focus on yourself and everything around you," said Skylar. "To control earth you must think like earth. Focus on the plants and the animals, the insects and the bugs, and everything

CHAPTER SEVEN

earth provides for. Focus on your breathing and close your eyes. Feel around you."

A small gust of wind blew across the grass, making it bend gracefully. A robin started singing cheerfully.

"Close your eyes. Focus," said Skylar.

Jason closed his eyes and tried to feel like earth. He imagined creatures crawling over him as insects walked on the earth every day. He tensed himself like a rock.

"Imagine yourself like grass, swaying in the wind," Skylar's voice sounded distant.

Jason imagined a large gust of wind flying over him, and tried to focus on the surrounding grass. The sound of rustling leaves filled his mind, nearly convincing him that he was in the middle of a forest.

"Focus," Skylar's gentle voice echoed out from the midst of the cacophony.

Jason filled his thoughts with the feeling and sound of earth. He thought of himself as a strong tree, his branches outstretched over a field of flowers. He imagined himself as a giant bird, flying over mountains taller than Evercliff, one of the tallest mountains in his Realm. All of a sudden he was a graceful stag, bounding over crevices and fox dens. His hooves turned into great, powerful paws, swiping at a beehive to get at the sweet honey inside. He was a tree again, his roots stretching over the hills, growing stronger and deeper.

"That's enough!" an echoing shadow of Skylar's voice interrupted him.

The tree's roots slowed down, and they started shrinking back into the earth.

"Jason, that's enough."

The tree started to morph into a boy. The roots started transforming into legs, the trunk carved itself into a human face. He stepped out from the tree, leaving a gaping hole where he had been. Blue eyes appeared in the face, small details revealing the identity of the boy.

"Jason?"

Jason opened his eyes. He was gasping and sweat was trickling into his eyes. Skylar was kneeling down next to, her eyes desperate.

"What happened?" asked Jason, wiping the sweat off his forehead.

"Didn't you hear me calling you?" said Skylar. She sounded angry, but Jason knew she was just desperately worried.

"No, I didn't," said Jason, fear and confusion grabbing hold of him.

"The grass started growing, but you weren't controlling the earth. It was controlling you."

"I was a tree and a–a bear and a bird."

"Calm down, Jason, calm down."

"Why was it doing that?" asked Jason, standing up. Roots that had been coiled around him shrunk back into the earth.

CHAPTER SEVEN

"It must have sensed that you had the power to control it, and it challenged you to see if you were strong enough. That's what it was doing, challenging you. It's all right; You didn't get hurt and neither did I–"

Skylar was cut short as a creature of fire flew into the clearing. Its wings were made of curling flames and its elegant head had sharp, piercing eyes that stared at Jason. Ember ran into the clearing and stopped at the edge of the grass, her hands on fire. They brushed against the grass, causing it to smoke.

"Is everyone okay?" asked Ember frantically.

"Yes. Ember, what happened?" asked Skylar worriedly.

"I heard you shouting Jason's name! I thought you two were in danger," said Ember, quenching the flames that had started curling up her arms.

"The earth was controlling him," said Skylar.

"Oh," said Ember, suddenly calm as she turned to Jason. "That happened to me my first time. I burnt down a whole field. In fact, I think I still owe the farmer."

Ember held her arm out to the bird of fire that was circling above her. The bird called out, a harsh chirp that echoed through the clearing. Once it had called out, it flew down and landed on Ember's outstretched arm.

"What kind of bird is it?" asked Jason, wondering if it would burn him if he tried to stroke it.

"First of all, it is a he," said Ember. "And secondly, to answer your question: he is a phoenix."

Skylar smiled.

"It has been a long time since you summoned him."

"I know," said Ember, glancing at Skylar. "He is usually very reluctant to come out. It must be his connection to Jason."

Jason looked up at his name and smiled shyly. Ember looked at him thoughtfully. Her eyes had turned a warm scarlet, the color of fire. Jason couldn't help but wonder what it was that made them change color like that; he had seen her do it a couple of times, but could never get used to the way her eyes melted from hazel to flaming red.

"Are you done with the lesson?" asked Ember abruptly.

"Yes, I think it would be too dangerous to try again. The earth would be more confident and would probably overwhelm Jason more easily than before," answered Skylar

Ember nodded. "Wise choice."

"Let's get going then?" said Skylar.

"Yes. I've looked around enough," said Ember.

She sent her phoenix away with a sweep of her arm. The bird died away slowly. The last flames dissolved with a mournful, echoing cry. Ember summoned her staff. The scarlet stone suspended between the branches was dull, as if it did not belong to this world. Skylar nodded to Ember. Jason barely had time to take one last look around before they all vanished from the Hidden Universe.

CHAPTER EIGHT

Challenges

"Come on, Jason," said Skylar.

"Coming," said Jason, standing up wearily.

It had been a week since the first lesson about earth. Every day since then, there had been two lessons a day, one at midday and one before they set up camp in the evening. Jason hadn't been getting any better at controlling the earth. It always saw his presence as a challenge and he always ended up losing control.

The constant moving from one place to another didn't help either, in fact it was tiring and distracting. His head ached after the lesson at midday, and when it was time for the evening lesson Jason's attempts got worse. There were some days when Jason was ready to give up, and although Skylar and Ember supported him and helped him in every way they could, it didn't seem to get any better.

"Here," said Ember, handing Jason a strong, staff-shaped stick. "If you get tired you can use it to walk."

"Thanks," said Jason, taking it gratefully.

Ember smiled and walked on ahead, her own staff in hand, the orb glowing warmly in the forest. It had been a few hours since lunch and the forest was preparing for night. The sun had almost set, and the first few stars were already twinkling in the sky. Jason sighed at the thought of the next lesson. He would undoubtedly fail to control the stubborn earth.

"Here is good," said Morpheus, leading them into a clearing.

"I suppose," said the Duchess, looking around the clearing with a look of distaste.

Jason looked at the Duchess out of the corner of his eye. The tiring week had taken more of a toll on her than on him. She was used to a life of luxury, and the continuous walking and changing camp had rendered her worse for the wear. The Duchess' usually silky hair lay in drab curls on her head. Her green eyes were rimmed red from the changing of the guard that Morpheus had organized to keep a constant lookout at night. Her furs still hung from her shoulders, but every effort to keep them clean had vanished.

The Duchess sat down at the foot of a tree and started unpacking the leftovers of the previous meal.

"Thank you, Duchess," said Skylar, unsmiling.

The Duchess nodded grimly without looking up.

"Should I start a fire?" Ember asked Skylar.

"Yes, thank you."

Ember started gathering some broken branches from the previous night's gale and Morpheus summoned the tents.

CHAPTER EIGHT

"Thank you, Morpheus," said Skylar, helping Ember with the branches.

"What can I do?" asked Jason.

"You can clear your mind for the next lesson, I think that would be best," said Skylar.

"Fine," said Jason bitterly, trying to rid his mind of all thoughts.

"Do not talk to me like that, Jason. This week has been hard on all of us, but you don't need to take that tone with me," said Skylar.

"Sorry," said Jason.

Jason sat down on the wet grass, thinking of how it had been covered in snow just the previous day. He sat cross-legged and closed his eyes. He felt the ground underneath him and imagined the rough bark of a tree. His mind filled with the sounds of a forest: the singing of the birds, the rustling of tree branches, and thousands of other peaceful sounds.

"Open your eyes, Jason," said Skylar.

Jason opened his eyes. He was once more in the field Ember had imagined when she had transported them to the Hidden Universe. Skylar sat across from him, her staff beside her.

"Remember what I told you this morning?" asked Skylar, her brows lifted inquiringly.

"Yes," said Jason, opening his fists.

"What did I tell you?"

"To relax," said Jason, lowering his gaze.

"That means you're not supposed to make fists," said Skylar.

"Sorry."

"Jason," said Skylar in a tone that made Jason look up. "Do you want to control the earth?"

"Yes," said Jason, surprising himself with the force with which he had answered.

"Then you need to do as I say. The Realms are counting on you, and that means you need to learn how to control the Elements as fast as possible."

"I know, and you've said this at least a thousand times. Haven't you even thought for one second if I want to be Keeper? Do you think I want hundreds of thousands of people counting on me? And if I fail then I'll be shamed forever, you won't be proud of me and now that I know about the Realms then I'll probably end up living here, and I won't have any friends or be accepted anywhere." Jason struggled not to stand up, his arms trembling at the force of angry energy.

"Jason, of course I've thought of these things. And of course I'll be proud of you whether you succeed or fail."

Skylar's words filled Jason's heart with a warm feeling, but the anger and resentment still simmered beneath the surface.

"I don't even care if you manage to control earth. To tell the truth, I'm angry at how hard this is for you. I'm angry that earth is hard on you, but that's what it does. Earth gives life, and in many of the Realms one thing they say a lot is that life is hard. It can

CHAPTER EIGHT

burn you down and crush your soul but it's not life that decides if you keep going. It's you."

"Thanks," said Jason.

"I'm always going to be here to support you, you know that."

"Yeah, I do."

"All right. Let's see you give it a shot."

Jason nodded and closed his eyes. Skylar's words were still fresh in his mind, giving him a newfound strength.

A creaking sound filled his ears, the sound of cracking wood. He imagined a branch waving wildly in the air, like a snake that was thrashing about. He felt his arms harden and his fingers grow into long, thin branches. Jason opened his eyes and forced himself not to panic at the sight of his branch-like arms.

"You're doing it, Jason!" said Skylar. "You're controlling the earth."

Jason smiled and looked down at his legs. They were turning into one, thick tree trunk. He grew as tall as a tree and towered over Skylar.

The branches swayed in the wind, and for a moment, Jason lost his concentration. The branch shrunk and turned into his arm again, then the same thing happened to his other arm. The trunk sank into the earth as it slowly changed back into his legs.

"That was awesome!" said Jason, when his legs had fully transformed.

"It was quite the transformation. Even Ember took longer than you, and she's the most exceptional student I have ever taught."

"What does Ember transform into?" asked Jason curiously. A new energy coursed through his veins.

"When it first happened, she was covered in fire and almost burnt the farmer's house down. I'm not sure if he's still hunting her or not."

"A farmer is hunting her?" asked Jason.

Skylar smiled good-humoredly. "I'm just kidding," she laughed.

Jason smiled. He wanted to cherish this new-found feeling of achievement.

"Should we go now? We can continue again tomorrow." asked Skylar.

"Yeah, let's go."

"We're not done yet, though," said Skylar, picking up her staff and standing up. "We need to practice doing it in real danger, and then we'll move on to air."

"Air? Does that mean I'll get to learn how to fly?" said Jason, following her lead.

"You can only control air if you absolutely trust it, but I'm sure you'll manage."

"Okay."

"Ready?" asked Skylar.

CHAPTER EIGHT

Jason nodded, thinking to himself that after turning into a tree he felt ready for anything.

"Let's go." Skylar touched the orb on her staff and the next second they were both back in the Realm.

"How was it?" asked Ember, sitting in her usual spot next to the fire.

"Perfect," said Skylar, with an unmistakable smile playing across her features. "He managed to turn into a tree."

"Do you think he will manage to turn into animals?" asked the Duchess, her dainty nose all red, and herself covered in blankets as though she had a cold.

"Are you all right, Duchess?" asked Skylar, worry flashing across her face.

"She got a cold while you were away. It's probably the Forest of Time doing it," said Ember.

"Time has sped up," said Morpheus, his face half hidden in the shadows of the trees.

"Anyway," said the Duchess, obviously annoyed with them talking about her cold. "Back to my question: do you think he will manage to turn into animals?"

"No," said Skylar and Ember in unison.

Skylar glanced at Ember and the latter nodded as if to say 'go ahead'.

"Earth -in the magical use of the word- involves only the plants," said Skylar.

The Duchess nodded and her gaze turned to the fire. Skylar sighed and glanced up at Morpheus as he spoke.

"Dinner is ready, by the way," said Morpheus from his corner. "Just so you know."

"Dinner is ready?" demanded the Duchess, standing up hastily. "I'm starving. Is there anything hot?"

"Yes, there's some soup, freshly heated up," said Morpheus.

"Perfect." said the Duchess, walking toward it with the ends of her blankets trailing on the ground.

"All right, I guess it's time to eat," said Skylar as she stood up and followed the Duchess.

"I'm not hungry," said Ember.

"Not hungry?" asked Skylar. "Are you feeling all right?"

"Yes, I'm fine," said Ember, with a faint but sad smile.

"Well, I'm hungry," said Jason, ready for a good meal.

Skylar glanced worriedly at Ember before starting to fill her bowl with soup. Jason did the same and so did Morpheus. The Duchess had already started eating.

Dinner was a quiet affair. The Duchess finished her bowl in seconds and decided to turn in for an early night. Morpheus took the first watch for the night and made himself comfortable at the top of a tree, in order to see intruders from far away. Ember remained quiet and stared at the flames of the fire. Vivid images would occasionally appear within the flames. Skylar and Jason sat next to the fire to enjoy some warmth before going to bed.

"You should go to bed, Jason," said Skylar.

"I know, but can't I stay up a bit?" asked Jason, feeling relaxed at the silence of the forest at night.

"No, we need to start early tomorrow, and you know that. We will also continue trying to control earth. It obviously gave in to you for some reason."

"I think it's because of what you said," said Jason. "And maybe it knew how I felt."

"It could be that," said Skylar. "But that does not mean we won't try again tomorrow, so go and get some sleep."

"Fine," said Jason, trying to control his tone.

"Goodnight," said Skylar.

"Goodnight," said Jason, as he stood up and entered his tent.

He snuggled down in his sleeping bag and made himself comfortable. The fire outside cast strange and ominous shapes on the walls of his tent. Jason knew he should try and get some sleep but watched the shadows for a bit, entranced by how similar to animals they looked. He dimly heard Skylar's voice and strained his ears to hear her.

"—of course I'm very proud of him for controlling the earth and am positive that it will gradually become easier for him...

can't help but worry... in battle. It will be completely different to a quiet field. Do you remember the Third World War? So many lives... before Invictius came to power. I just can't imagine the pressure... once they come face to... like the Third World War all over again."

"Calm down, Skylar," said Ember, speaking so low Jason had to lean against the tent to hear her properly. "Jason will... Realms will be fine too. You have nothing to worry about."

"I suppose," said Skylar. Her voice was calm but a trace of worry still remained. "I just don't know what I would do if he got hurt."

At this, Jason lay back down in his sleeping bag. Skylar's words had somehow seared a hole in his heart. Even he couldn't imagine the pressure that was on him. If the Realms were to be destroyed it would all be his fault. Just thinking about it made his chest hurt. With these thoughts pounding in his head, Jason drifted off into troublesome dreams.

* * *

Jason awoke to the sound of rain on canvas and the drip drop as it fell through the branches of the trees. He yawned loudly and got out of the sleeping bag. The outside world looked wet and uninviting.

"Perfect," muttered Jason sarcastically.

Jason stepped out of the tent and stretched his arms. Ember was already awake and was sitting next to the remains of the fire.

"Where is everyone else?" asked Jason as he approached her.

CHAPTER EIGHT

"Morpheus went to bed at four this morning, to get some sleep before we start walking. And Skylar and the Duchess are still asleep."

"Morpheus had to keep watch all night?" asked Jason.

"Yep," said Ember, uninterested.

"What's up?" asked Jason, noticing her moody tone.

Ember raised her eyebrows. "What's up? Is that how you talk in your Realm?"

"Um, yeah? I just wanted to ask why you've been so moody lately."

"Oh. I guess it's because I've been reminded of my home."

"Where is your home?"

"In another place. Far away."

"Jason," said Skylar from behind him. "I think you should leave Ember to her own thoughts."

Jason turned around. "Oh, sorry."

"You don't owe an apology to me," said Skylar.

"Right," said Jason, turning to face Ember. "Sorry, Ember."

"It's fine... Keeper."

Jason smiled at her comment and looked down at the black stones that used to be a fire. He heard a pair of footsteps coming toward him. Skylar sat down next to him. The Duchess emerged from her tent and yawned loudly. She was an even bigger mess than the night before. Her hair was in a drab bun that hung lopsidedly. Her furs were trailing on the ground, the bright white of them having turned brown.

"Wow," said Ember in surprise. "Are you okay, Duchess?"

"Yes," said the Duchess in a husky voice. "I'm perfectly fine."

The Duchess sneezed ferociously and sat down next to Ember. Her nose was strawberry red, and with her brown furs wrapped around her neck, it reminded Jason of a reindeer he had heard stories about. Ember was struggling to keep a straight face; the same thought must have occurred to her too.

"Do you want some tea, Duchess?" asked Skylar worriedly, glaring at Ember for a second.

"That would be — achoo — most welcome," said the Duchess.

Skylar nodded and started preparing the water. Ember caught Jason's eye and smiled, probably still thinking about the Duchess and her furs.

Morpheus came walking out of the forest. He was easily the most dignified of the party. He wore a blue and golden cloak that fluttered around him. His goatee was as trim as ever. Along with the golden staff he always held, it was quite an astonishing sight to behold.

"Ah, making tea are we?" asked Morpheus quite cheerfully, considering he had been up all night.

CHAPTER EIGHT

"Yes — achoo — Skylar is making it for me," said the Duchess, possibly thinking that Morpheus was planning on taking some.

"Yes, yes. I can see that you probably should have it," said Morpheus, sitting down across from Ember. Her gaze immediately turned to stone.

"Here you are," said Skylar, handing the Duchess a mug of steaming tea. "I did tell you that it would be better if you didn't come, though."

"Yes, you did," said the Duchess after taking a sip. "But I thought I should keep an eye on you."

"Of course," muttered Skylar under her breath.

"Could I have some hot chocolate?" asked Jason.

"Actually, I think we should get going," said Morpheus. "I went and cleared the path we took yesterday, and I think we should keep as much distance between us and the Kingdom as possible."

"I agree," said Skylar.

"Fine," said the Duchess in her husky voice. "I suppose we should get going."

"Don't you have magical medicine for her?" asked Jason, turning to Skylar at the sound of the Duchess' voice.

"Well yes, I do, but I left it at home."

"I brought some," said Ember.

"You brought some? But you never get sick," said Skylar.

"I thought we might need it."

"All right, go and get some then," said Skylar.

Ember excused herself and went running back to her tent. She came back a few seconds later, carrying silver colored packets filled with powder.

"There you go," said Skylar, pouring some powder in the Duchess' tea.

"Thank you," said the Duchess, taking a sip.

"Let's get going, then," said Morpheus, standing up. "Skylar, prepare some toast for the road. I will start packing the tents."

Skylar nodded and got to work making toast. Morpheus made the tents disappear and came back to remove the scorched stones from the fireplace. The Duchess finished her tea with a satisfied face. Her nose wasn't as red, and she no longer sneezed. She cleaned her furs with her staff and tied her hair in a braid.

Soon they were back on the road. With the singing of the birds and the tree branches above his head, Jason was reminded of how he had controlled the earth the previous day. He found himself desperately hoping he would succeed again.

After a long morning of walking, Morpheus finally signaled to them to stop for lunch. The Duchess sighed and sat down. Skylar immediately started getting lunch ready and asked Ember to prepare a fire. Before long, the air was filled with the smell of hot soup and the crackling of a cheerful fire.

An ominous sound of cracking twigs suddenly echoed throughout the forest. Skylar stopped her task and looked up, startled.

CHAPTER EIGHT

Morpheus, too, stopped what he was doing and looked in the direction of the disturbing sound. Skylar signaled to Morpheus and slowly hid behind a tree trunk. Morpheus and Ember did the same, while staying as quiet as possible. The Duchess grabbed Jason's wrist and pushed him behind a stone. With a glance at Skylar, she moved next to him.

A giant roar rang out among the trees. Jason shivered to think what creature could have made such a loud noise. There was a moment of silence, the quiet before the storm.

A gigantic, horrifying yet graceful creature entered the clearing. The creature's head was that of an eagle. Large, yellow eyes looked around as it clicked its beak angrily. The creature's feathers spread down its chest and over its wings, stopping at its back. As the feathers ended, they were replaced by fur. Amber-colored fur that swept over the rest of its back and stomach. The creature had a tail that it held above the ground. Jason recognized it to be the tail of a lion. The creature's front legs were like the claws of a bird and the hind paws were those of a lion.

"Griffin," said the Duchess, obviously terrified.

"What's a griffin?" asked Jason, whispering out of pure fear.

"Savage creatures that roam in forests. They're almost impossible to kill." The regal tone had disappeared from the Duchess' voice.

Jason looked in Skylar's direction. She had summoned her staff. Her knuckles were white from the strength with which she was gripping it. Jason saw her give a signal to Morpheus, who nodded. Ember watched them from her own hiding place. She hadn't summoned her staff, instead she held a ball of fire in her hand. Though it looked like she was ready for a fight, Jason noticed the shadow of a smile flash across her features. Confused by this, he looked back at Skylar. She was signaling with her hand: three... two... one!

Skylar exploded out from behind the trunk. She held her staff high and shot a spell in the direction of the griffin. It ricocheted off the creature's wings, obviously protected by some type of magic. The creatures reared up on its hind legs and produced a furious roar that made the ground tremble.

"Morpheus!" cried Skylar.

Morpheus shot out from behind the trunk and sent a spell flying in the direction of the griffin. He grabbed Skylar's arm and shoved her behind a boulder. The griffin swiped at Morpheus with his talons. Morpheus turned just in time and held up his staff. The creature was pushed away by Morpheus' protective shield. As the griffin stood up, Ember made as if to step out from behind the tree trunk.

"No, Ember!" shouted Skylar. "Stay where you are!"

Ember shot her a look and settled back down. The ball of fire in her hand grew ever so slightly. Morpheus turned at Skylar's voice, and just then the griffin took its chance and swiped at him. Morpheus shouted out and grasped his shoulder with his hand. Small drops of blood dripped from between his fingers, staining his hand and sleeve.

"Morpheus! Come here!" said Skylar, inching toward him.

Morpheus took a couple of steps toward the edge of the clearing. His eyes rolled back in his head, and he collapsed on the ground. The griffin roared over Skylar's cries and ran toward her.

CHAPTER EIGHT

"No!" shouted Ember, shooting out from behind the trunk.

A red shield of fire surrounded Skylar as Ember cried out. The griffin stepped back and roared again. The ball of fire in Ember's hand transformed into a gleaming sword made of fire. Ember struck at the griffin's legs. The creature cried out as the sword pierced its skin, burning a deep cut in its leg. The griffin turned to face Ember, his strong tail making contact with her head. She barely had time to cry out before she collapsed to the ground. Jason tried to run forward as the griffin turned back to Skylar. The Duchess caught his arm and pushed him back behind the stone.

"I will help, you stay here."

The Duchess ran out in the open and shouted at the griffin to get its attention. The griffin spotted her waving her arms like a madman and aimed for her. The Duchess summoned her staff and shot a spell toward its face. It didn't seem to do anything. The griffin just kept coming. The Duchess stumbled backward and fell on the ground next to Morpheus. She glanced at him, terror showing in her eyes. The Duchess shot a plasma blast at the griffin. The spell slowed the creature down, but that was all. The griffin took a last step toward her until it was upon her. The Duchess closed her eyes, preparing herself for the worst.

"No!!!"

The word echoed in the clearing. The griffin froze and looked toward Jason, who stood in plain sight. The creature knew that the real battle was just about to begin.

Curling vines shot out of the ground. They wrapped themselves around Morpheus and Ember and laid them behind the same stone where Jason had been just seconds before. Jason gestured up with his hand. A vine curled around the griffin's neck.

Tighter and tighter, strangling the creature until it drifted into unconsciousness and fell to the ground. Other vines shot up from the earth and caught hold of the griffin's hind paws and deadly talons. The griffin twitched in its sleep but settled back down. The vines finished tying the griffin to the ground, going around and around its legs and securing the griffin in place.

Jason sighed in relief and stumbled toward a tree. He caught hold of a branch to steady himself. His legs were trembling, and he struggled not to faint. Jason looked at the griffin. One of its claws was pointing in his direction. It reminded him of someone drawing their thumb across their neck. An ominous sign, but hopefully one that meant nothing. Just then Jason noticed the Duchess staring at him, her mouth open in surprise. Jason saw a trace of fear in her eyes, but the Duchess quickly hid it. Jason looked at Skylar: she too was looking at him, but she was smiling wider than Jason had ever seen her smile before. Jason smiled nervously, he hadn't been completely sure what the outcome would be. Yes, he had saved all of their lives, but were there rules that applied to fighting? Had he unknowingly broken them?

"That was... smart," said the Duchess, wincing at her own compliment.

Skylar laughed and ran forward. She drew Jason into her arms in a tight embrace.

"That was wonderful, dear! You managed to control earth under pressure," said Skylar, kissing his forehead tenderly.

"Yes, he did," said the Duchess, standing up shakily. "It was truly wonderful."

Skylar laughed again and planted a last kiss on Jason's head.

CHAPTER EIGHT

"We will have a celebratory lunch. Duchess, could you wake up Morpheus and Ember? Sprinkle them with waking powder."

The Duchess nodded, obviously pleased to have something to do that would distract her from the giant body of the griffin, sprawled in the middle of the clearing. She rummaged inside one of the packs and drew out a small bag, then poured its contents over Ember's face. Ember coughed and sat up. She felt the side of her head, feeling around the bump with a slight grimace. The Duchess walked over to Morpheus and did the same thing again. He sneezed and felt his arm. His pain could easily be seen in his eyes.

"Are you all right?" asked Skylar, already lighting a fire.

"What happened?" asked Morpheus, clenching his jaw as if to block out the pain building in his arm.

"The griffin struck you. Don't worry though, I'll make some tea with healing powder in it."

"I could heal him," said Ember, dropping her hand from her head.

"No, you're too weak to draw power from your soul. I think it would be better if we use healing powder," said Skylar, now busy with filling the kettle with water.

"All right," said Ember, lying back down on the ground.

"Here," said the Duchess, bringing some ice to Ember. "Put this on your head."

"Do you want me to bandage your arm, Morpheus?" asked Skylar.

"Yes," said Morpheus, letting out a grunt as another bout of pain ran through his arm. "That would be most welcome."

"Jason," said Skylar.

"Yes?"

"In that pack over there, there should be a magical first aid kit, get it and bring it to me, please."

"Okay."

Jason rushed forward and rummaged through the indicated pack. He pushed aside a blanket and found a small, leather bag. In golden letters, on the side, it said 'first aid kit'. Jason grabbed it and ran to Skylar.

"Here it is," said Jason, handing the bag to her.

"Thank you, Jason," said Skylar, hurrying to Morpheus, her violet cloak flapping around her.

Skylar kneeled down at Morpheus' side. She opened the bag and took out a roll of dressing. She looked inside the bag again and brought out a small bottle with swirling, golden liquid inside. Skylar poured some of the golden liquid on Morpheus' wound. He groaned softly as the magical medicine stung tender flesh.

"Sorry," whispered Skylar.

Morpheus nodded as if to say 'do what you have to do'. Skylar paused a second to let him relax again, then unrolled the dressing. She wrapped it around Morpheus' arm and secured it with tape.

CHAPTER EIGHT

"All right. It should heal by tonight," said Skylar, as she put the roll back in the bag and stood up.

"Thank you, Skylar," said Morpheus.

"It was nothing."

Skylar smiled and put the magical kit back in the pack. Morpheus stood up shakily and sat down next to the fire. His hand still shaking, he was barely able to hold the mug of tea Skylar had given him. Ember had gone to sit next to the fire while Skylar had taken care of Morpheus' wound. The mark the griffin had left on Ember's forehead had vanished. Jason leaned against a tree. His eyes were closed, and he was deep in thought, replaying in his mind the battle against the griffin. The Duchess was sitting on a log. She stared into nothingness, and Jason thought he could sense her fear cloak her like a cold whisper in her mind.

"Are you all right, Luna?" asked Skylar, sitting down beside the Duchess and touching her shoulder.

"Where did the griffin come from?" said the Duchess, a terrible fear flashing in her eyes as she looked at Skylar. "Where did it come from?"

Skylar glanced at Ember. A brief, vague expression passed over her face.

"What do you know?" the Duchess asked Ember.

Ember stared back at her, her face inexpressible. Only a small hint of laughter could be seen in her eyes.

"The griffin is actually one of the pets of the king," said Ember.

Her words shook Jason from his daydream. "We actually sent him here to attack us."

"You did what?" asked the Duchess incredulously.

"To see if Jason could control his powers in battle," said Skylar calmly.

"What?" asked Jason, a boiling fury starting to rise in his chest. "I was terrified! I was scared that you were going to die, and everyone else too!"

Ember laughed aloud. Jason froze in surprise at the surprising melody of her laughter.

"What are you laughing at?" asked Jason, embarrassed.

"Your reaction, obviously," said Ember. Jason's face turned red. "Just the fact that you underestimate us like that is funny."

"But... what about your head?" asked Jason.

"Oh, that was real. But Bob knows I heal myself, so it's fine," said Ember, still smiling.

"Bob?" asked Jason, aware that everyone was looking at him.

"That's the griffin's name," said Ember.

Jason fell silent, feeling slightly bitter at Ember's words. He didn't underestimate them, he felt responsible for them. Even responsible for Ember's safety.

CHAPTER NINE

The Sacred Temples of the Ancient

Onyx rose high above the trees. Her wings beat fiercely to give her the boost she needed. Finding nothing worthy of her attention, she lowered herself to the ground.

"Did you find anything?" asked the Alpha, looking around the recent campground with contempt.

"No, if they were here they are long gone now," said Onyx, holding her bow tightly.

Onyx and the Alpha had been traveling for a week, looking and searching for any signs of where the boy could be. They had only found his trail a couple of days ago. But their prey had always been one step ahead. Onyx walked over to the remains of a campfire. There were only a few scorched stones, the only signs of any fire. Onyx bent down and touched the embers; they were cold. Her eyes swept the clearing again. There were no other traces of a recent camp.

"They are probably well ahead of us by now," said the Alpha, his words rolling out in a growl. "We will never catch up."

"We need to," answered Onyx. "Or Invictius will have our heads."

"Why don't you call him lord? Or the master?" asked the Alpha. "We should respect him. He will get rid of all the injustice in the Realms."

"Who said I want that?" said Onyx angrily. "He tore me away from my family. My tribe. I never said I wanted him to murder villages and cities. All I want is to be free from his grasp."

"You know that that is impossible. Lord Invictius would never let you go."

"I know, but I will try. Then I will never have to see his face again. I will finally be rid of his awful, human stench."

"Though he is human, he is powerful," said the Alpha, sniffing around, trying to get a lead on his prey.

"I know, that's why I hate him so much."

The Alpha growled.

"What? Did you find something?" asked Onyx urgently, hurrying to his side with a flap of her wings.

"This way," said the Alpha.

"Finally. We're back on the trail," said Onyx,

The Alpha howled in satisfaction. Onyx beat her wings to rise into the air. With the wind in her hair she headed north. Toward the Sacred Temples of the Ancient.

* * *

Jason stumbled forward. He felt the weeks' worth of walking

CHAPTER NINE

taking a toll on him. His legs suddenly felt like jelly, and he felt as though he could barely stand.

"Are you all right, Jason?" asked Ember, who was walking behind him.

"Yes, yes. I'm good," said Jason, glancing behind him at Ember, faking a happy smile.

"Okay. If you're sure."

"Yeah, I'm good."

Jason forced his legs to stop trembling and kept walking forward. He leaned on his stick with all his weight and with a last effort, he walked another hundred meters, then collapsed onto a stone. Morpheus and Skylar, who were ahead of him, stopped and hurried back to him.

"Jason, if you're too tired we can stop tonight, and arrive there tomorrow instead," said Skylar, helping him sit up properly.

"No. I want to get there today," said Jason immediately. "I want to get there today, so then all of this is over as fast as possible."

"All right," said Skylar. "But if you want to stop for the night just tell me. You defeated the griffin yesterday, and I completely understand if you're too tired to go on."

"Yeah. Bob," said Jason with a faint smile on his lips. "I don't want to meet him again. But no, I want to get there today."

"All right," said Skylar. "If you're sure."

"Completely sure."

"Shall we get going, then?" asked the Duchess, leaning against one of the few trees in their surroundings.

"All right," said Morpheus. "Come on then." He started leading the way up the mountain.

To keep his mind off the strain building up in his legs, Jason fixed his attention on the scenery. A few hours ago, the dense forest they had been walking through for the past week had changed to a steep hill with sparse trees. The Forest of Time had been left behind to make way to cold, bitter frost and horrible gales. They had been walking uphill for a day, trying to get to the midpoint of the mountain they were climbing. In the Forest of Time Jason had rarely seen birds, but here, in the middle of nowhere, golden-feathered birds occasionally flew high above them.

"Stop," said Morpheus urgently.

Skylar blocked Jason's path with her arm. He peered over her shoulder curiously. A seemingly infinite gorge stood in their path. The darkness of the depths went on forever.

"The Infinite Fall," said the Duchess in a squeaky voice.

"Yes, this is definitely it," said Morpheus, looking carefully into its depths.

Jason tried to get a good measure of the gorge's size. Ember tossed a ball of fire into the gorge. They could see the flames only for a few seconds, before its weak light was engulfed by the shadows.

"How do we pass?" Skylar asked Morpheus.

"The legends say that there should be a lever or something.

CHAPTER NINE

You need to press the sun on the cross," answered Morpheus, looking around.

"There," said the Duchess, as she noticed the circle engraved on a cross shaped tree.

"Perfect," said Morpheus, pressing the circle.

A flash of blinding light connected the two sides of the gorge. It remained for a second, before slowly filtering away.

"How do we know the bridge is there?" asked Skylar, hesitantly stepping forward to the edge of the gorge.

"The ideal thing would be a rock or a stick," said Ember, picking up a fist sized stone.

"Give it to me," said Morpheus insistently.

Ember gave it to him. In her haste she forgot to show any sign of hostility. Morpheus threw the rock. A resounding thud rang through the air. The Duchess sighed in relief and almost took the first step. Morpheus signaled to her to wait and went first instead. There was a collective moment of relief when Morpheus took a step and didn't fall.

Skylar took Jason's hand and they stepped on the bridge. Jason felt a moment of fear and exhilaration as he walked across to the other side. He could see the black nothingness below him and thought this must be what it felt like to fly.

Soon after, everyone was on the other side of the gorge. Skylar took the lead. Everyone followed her up the side of the mountain. Finally, after what seemed like forever, they reached the entrance to the Sacred Temples of the Ancient. Two tall stone pillars, with enough space between them for a horse to pass between.

"Alright," said Skylar. "Morpheus first, then the Duchess, then Jason, then Ember, and last of all me."

They nodded in agreement. Skylar moved out of the way of the entrance to let Morpheus go first. Morpheus gave a last glance at everyone and stepped through. He disappeared through an invisible portal. The entrance shimmered in the sunlight like the ripple of water in a lake. Skylar nodded to the Duchess. There was a moment of silence in which the Duchess hesitated, but at last she stepped through the portal. The Duchess disappeared just like Morpheus. Without a second of hesitation, Jason plunged himself into the portal.

He felt himself grow dizzy, as if he were whirling round and round in a whirlpool. The motion gradually stopped. He steadied himself, and slowly his surroundings came into focus.

Jason gasped as a scenery that could rival a fairy tale passage unfolded before him. It was a valley surrounded by mountains. Silver and golden trees cloaked the land like a blanket. From the top of the mountain he was on, he could see the whole Great Lake. Rainbow-colored flowers were scattered across the land beneath the mountains. All of these things were equally beautiful, but the one thing that stole Jason's attention the longest were the Temples. Nine Temples, each the size of a small mansion, stood in a row in the middle of the valley. It looked like a gigantic rainbow in the middle of a field.

"Wow," said someone behind Jason. He turned around. Ember was looking at the Temples as if she couldn't believe they were actually there.

CHAPTER NINE

"They're just as I remember," said Skylar, stepping out of the shimmering portal.

"Come here! Now!" shouted Morpheus' voice from out of sight, just behind a rock.

Skylar, Ember and Jason rushed forward, using Morpheus' voice as a guide. As soon as possible they had come to his side, and to a horrifying sight. The Duchess was suspended in the air by curling, snapping, giant flesh-eating Venus flytraps. She looked sad and helpless, and she was unconscious.

"How did this happen?" asked Skylar, summoning her staff.

"We came out of the portal, then they grabbed her and brought her here," said Morpheus, his own staff already in hand.

"It must be a kind of defense. Maybe it needs to be shown a Gifted power," said Ember, flames curling up her arm.

"I'll do it," said Jason, already trying to make contact with the earth.

"No," said Skylar, putting out her hand to stop him. "Ember can throw a ball of fire at it."

Ember looked at her in surprise. Jason saw the flames curling up Ember's neck diminish, as if they were mirroring her thoughts.

"Go on," said Skylar urgently, as the vines around the Duchess tightened.

Ember nodded and threw a ball of fire at the foot of the vines. They let go of the Duchess and slowly started snaking away. Morpheus caught the Duchess before she hit the ground and laid her on the floor. Skylar nodded to Ember, who understood and touched the Duchess. She coughed violently. Skylar and Morpheus helped her stand up.

"What happened?" asked the Duchess, trying to focus on her surroundings.

"You were knocked out by one of the vines," said Morpheus.

"My head hurts," said the Duchess, feeling around her head.

"Yes, that will leave soon." said Ember, her hand still touching the Duchess' arm.

"That's better," said the Duchess in relief.

Ember withdrew her hand and glanced at Jason. He was watching her in silent fury. He couldn't believe Skylar hadn't let him save the Duchess. Instead, she had chosen Ember. Jason watched Ember out of the corner of his eye. She seemed nervous, and there was no sign of a smug face about saving the Duchess.

"All right, we should probably head to the temples before it gets dark," said Skylar.

"Yes, that is probably the best thing we can do," said Morpheus, looking worried.

"Let's go then," said the Duchess.

It was a short journey to the Temples, but a very tiring one. It took about an hour to get down from the mountain. As soon as they had come to the foot of the mountain, Ember hurried to prepare a fire, and Skylar the food.

CHAPTER NINE

"What kind of Temples are there, Morpheus?" asked Ember, busy with organizing the kindling.

"There are nine Temples," answered Morpheus, helping to prepare the food, "based on the nine Gifted powers: the Stone Temple of earth, the Wind Temple of air, the Aqua Temple of water, the Flame Temple of fire, the Frozen Temple of ice, the Storm Temple of lightning, the Dark Temple of shadows, the Temple of Prophecies of time. And the Mind Temple of telepathy and mind reading."

"Those are a lot of temples," said the Duchess, pulling her furs around her neck as protection from the cold.

"Yes, but that is only what the legends say. I have never actually been here. The only one among us that has been here once before is Skylar," said Morpheus.

Everyone's eyes turned to Skylar, who was finished with the food and was sitting down next to everyone else. She looked away from them as their faces turned toward her. She gazed into the distance longingly.

"After," said Skylar.

* * *

After dinner, Jason stood up and said goodnight to everyone. For a few minutes, the rustling of a sleeping bag could be heard from the direction of his tent. But finally silence fell, a sure sign that Jason had fallen asleep. The Guardians gathered around the fire were quiet until all of a sudden conversations broke out once again.

"When did you come here?" asked Ember quietly. "You never told me before."

"A long time ago," said Skylar. "It was during the Third World War. I was wounded. Luna had betrayed me, Vic had betrayed me. I came here with my sister; we had known one of the first Gifted, and he had given us the location of the Temples. We knew it was the only place we could be safe."

The Duchess winced when Skylar mentioned her name.

"Vic..." said Ember. "Invictius?"

Skylar nodded. "Yes. It was my nickname for him. It was everyone's nickname for him. He was very likable, and everyone was friends with him. During a battle in the Third World War he was fighting at my side, but he disappeared in the middle of the battle. I thought he was wounded, or dead. But we saw each other another time. In the middle of a different battle. He was on the opposite side this time. And he was more powerful than ever."

"He was a Gifted, wasn't he?" asked Ember.

"Yes, he had the Gifted power of shadows," said Skylar.

A long silence followed her words. Everyone was too nervous to speak and kept glancing at the towering silhouette of the Temples.

"We should go to sleep," said Skylar.

The Duchess nodded and retreated to her tent without a word. Morpheus bid Skylar and Ember adieu and went to his own tent. Eventually, only Skylar and Ember were left at the side of the fire.

CHAPTER NINE

"Don't stay up too late, okay?" said Skylar, entering her own tent.

Ember watched her go, and then looked back at the Temples. Their size made them look close, but Ember knew they were farther than she thought. She had an urge to go and find the Flame Temple, the only place she knew she belonged. Ember shook the thought away. It wouldn't do to abandon Jason now. She would just have to wait until morning. Ember cast a last lingering look toward the Temples and decided to take Skylar's advice. With the thought of the Temples still in her mind, she went to sleep.

* * *

Jason awoke at the break of dawn. He hadn't closed the entrance to his tent properly, allowing the morning sunlight to filter through a small gap. Jason yawned and stretched his back. His legs felt tired and numb from the walking they had done yesterday, yet energy coursed through his veins. Jason got dressed and exited his tent.

Everyone else was already sitting around the fire eating breakfast. Skylar kept stoking the fire every few seconds, even though she had food on her lap and was eating. Ember couldn't keep still, and would either glance at the Temples after a bite of toast, or would make vivid images appear in the fire, startling Skylar whenever she turned to stoke it. The Duchess was continuously readjusting her furs and rearranging her hair into a braid or a bun. Morpheus had finished breakfast and was sitting beside the fire polishing his staff, but he kept glancing up in anticipation, a sure sign that he was nervous.

Skylar finished stoking the fire for the fourth time and looked up as Jason approached her. Ember glanced his way but other than that made no sign she had seen him. The Duchess was far too busy re-braiding her hair and didn't even look up. As for Morpheus, he seemed wholly concentrated on cleaning his staff.

"Good morning, dear," said Skylar with a smile.

"Good morning," said Jason. The second he opened his mouth, everyone else looked up in unison. "What?"

"Well, we're all very eager about today," said Skylar, stoking the fire again, "it's the second time I've been here and I'm as excited as the first time. As for everyone else, well, I'm sure they're very nervous to be walking in the footsteps of the first Gifted."

"There's more to it than that," said Jason, as Skylar glanced at Morpheus, who was back at work polishing his staff.

Skylar looked down at the fire, confirming Jason's thoughts. No-one was looking away from him now. They were looking at everyone but him.

"What happened?" asked Jason insistently.

"Well, dear," said Skylar, looking up at him. "it's just that among the first Gifted, there was also the Keeper, who technically owned the Sacred Temples of the Ancient. He was the most powerful person of the century, and he gathered the Gifted together to make the Temples. Of course, they didn't make the Temples like Nolmans do; they used their magic. But the point is, the Temples belong to the Keeper."

"Wait. Are you saying the Temples belong to me?" asked Jason disbelievingly.

"Yes," said Skylar.

CHAPTER NINE

Jason looked toward the Temples. In the sunlight they looked as majestic and elegant as they had bathed in moonlight. With their shimmering lights, and the crystal windows, they shone brighter than anything else in the valley. He couldn't believe they were actually his. It was like a dream he hadn't realized he had ever had.

"You've got to be kidding. I couldn't even dream of owning something like that," said Jason incredulously.

"No, Jason, I can assure you we're not kidding," said the Duchess with a twinkle in her eyes. "Also, I don't kid."

Jason laughed and hugged Skylar. Already this day had started amazingly. He couldn't wait to see how the rest of the day would turn out. Morpheus looked down at his staff and started polishing it again, although Jason could already see his own reflection in it, staring back at him. Ember stood up and gave Jason a fleeting smile, but her attention wandered elsewhere as she cleaned up the camp. The Duchess handed some toast to Jason before cleaning the breakfast dishes up and sending them back to the kitchens in the castle of the Crystal Kingdom. Skylar helped her, though she avoided looking at the Duchess.

"All right," said Skylar, with a sigh of satisfaction. "We've finished putting everything away, now who wants to go visit the Temples?"

Of course it was a rhetorical question. At her words, Jason shouldered his pack, and everyone else summoned their staffs.

"Let's get going then," said Skylar, as she started leading the way to the Temples.

the Keeper of the Elements

CHAPTER TEN

Wolves

Invictius threw a jug at the wall. The loud clanging of metal on stone resonated throughout the underground dining room as the jug crashed into the wall.

"I must know where he is!" Invictius demanded of Xander's cowering form.

"Yes," said Xander. "Of course, my lord, but Onyx has not sent word of where she is, or where she thinks the boy is going."

"I don't care!" shouted Invictius again. He stepped forward, making Xander take a step back. "All I care about is having the boy captured, and how can I know if he's been captured if that Shadow Wing does not tell me?"

"Yes, lord, but as I told you before, we do not know where she is."

"Then find out where she is," said Invictius threateningly.

"Yes, lord, of course, my lord," said Xander, bowing his head.

"Then leave!" said Invictius, throwing a crystal glass on the floor. Sadly, it was not the dramatic effect he had hoped for, as all it did was roll along the floor. "And don't dare come back if you don't find her."

"Yes, lord," said Xander as he turned away and practically fled from the room.

"I swear, Onyx," said Invictius to himself, once Xander's hurried clawed steps had faded from earshot. "If you don't send a message by tomorrow, I'll have you hunted down by Alpha and his pack."

Invictius looked down at the stone table. There was still part of his breakfast left untouched, though now there was no jug or glass. Invictius sighed and sat down on his wooden seat. Corvina squawked as she flew down from the rafters and perched on Invictius' arm.

"Hello, dear one," said Invictius lovingly, as he stroked the raven's head.

Corvina croaked again and settled back down with her eyes closed. Invictius became lost in his thoughts as he continued stroking the raven. He thought of finally having the boy and finally finding a way to steal the Keeper's Gifts. It made him angry to think of destiny choosing to give the Keeper's abilities to a boy. These thoughts made Invictius curl up his fist with a wave of furious anger that could not be tamed. Like a wild beast that would strike out when it got the chance.

Invictius looked up as the sound of light footsteps caught his attention. He glanced at his raven, but she was still perched on his arm. Invictius noticed her eyes were focused on something else though. Something that was entering the dining room through the door. Invictius followed her gaze with his eyes. A black wolf slinked through the arched entrance. The creature growled when

CHAPTER TEN

it saw that Invictius had noticed him.

"Ah, finally," said Invictius, standing up. "Do you have a letter from Onyx?"

The wolf growled softly and lifted its head, showing his neck and revealing a letter tied around it with a vine.

"Perfect," said Invictius, snapping the vine as he snatched the letter.

My lord, this is Onyx.

I know what you would say, I probably shouldn't write my name in a letter.
But I don't care.
I hope you're having a horrible day, and yes, I sent this letter late on purpose. Alpha and I have been traveling for almost ten days, there is still no sign of the boy or the Guardians with him, but we have been following a faint trail they left. I think they are going to the Sacred Temples of the Ancient, at least that is what it looks like.
The impostor is in place for the plan.
Again I don't care what you say.

Sending you my worst wishes,
Onyx

Invictius threw the letter on the floor impatiently. He didn't expect anything less from Onyx, but it wouldn't do to have her insult him. It might give the other prisoners ideas. Invictius started pacing the room. Onyx was doing a fine job, but she would need to hurry up. It wouldn't do to have the boy reach the Temples before she caught up with him. And what if the boy had already reached the Temples? Would he discover their secrets? Would he take the Temple's power for his own?

Invictius was shaken from his thoughts by a rude growl from the wolf. He was still in the room and was sitting down expectantly.

"What do you want?" demanded Invictius savagely. "A treat?"

The wolf whimpered as though he were asking for something.

"Get out."

The wolf growled and left the room, giving Invictius a greedy-eyed stare before he disappeared from sight. Invictius shot the wolf a look of hatred before pacing the room again.

* * *

Jason stumbled forward and grabbed hold of Skylar's arm to stop himself from falling face-first onto the muddy ground. He looked at her face to see a smile there that he knew meant there was something utterly beautiful in front of her. He followed her gaze and saw the most majestic thing he had ever seen. Before Jason were the Temples. He couldn't help but gasp at the beauty that lay before him.

On his far right was the Flame Temple. It was made of ruby, engraved with curling flames that rose up to the roof. They were so realistic that it looked as though a fire were surrounding the Temple. The crackling sound of burning wood came from within the Temple. The Temple itself was on fire. Situated near the entrance were two phoenixes sculpted out of ruby. The feathers were carved to the smallest detail, and their heads were wreathed in flames.

Beside the Flame Temple was the Aqua Temple. It was made of turquoise, and instead of flames engraved on the gemstone, there were waves of water. Just like in the ocean, they rose up threateningly and majestically. Amidst the engravings were bold lines that formed the silhouettes of two dolphins, one on either side of the entrance. The dolphins moved and swam along the walls. It was so realistic and finely made that Jason could almost feel the waves sweep under his legs, making him fall to the floor.

Next to the Aqua Temple, by a tunnel, was the Frozen Temple. The Frozen Temple was made entirely of diamonds, and looked almost exactly like ice sparkling in the morning sunlight. There were cracks in the diamond. And it could have been Jason's imagination, but when he drew close to the Temple, he felt a shiver run through him. Ermine statues stood next to the entrance. They rose on their rear legs and bared their teeth in a way that was almost unbecoming of such a gentle-looking creature.

Beside the Frozen Temple, was the Temple of Prophecies. The Temple of Prophecies was made of purple marble. Prophecies were engraved on the marble, hundreds of them. Whenever a new prophecy was made, it would appear engraved on the marble wall of the Temple, while the old prophecies would just fade away. Next to the entrance were two marble pedestals. On each pedestal was an owl.

The darkest Temple of them all was the Dark Temple, or the Temple of Shadows. It stood at the center of the nine Temples and stood out from the bright colors of the other Temples with its black hue. The Temple was made of plain stone set with black opal gems. The colors of the other Temples reflected in the sparkling surface of the stones. The symbolic animal of the shadows was a black cat. The head of the cat protruded from the stone. The whiskers and eyes were finely carved and the magic surrounding the Temple made it look like the cat was watching their every movement with its unnerving black eyes.

Next to the Dark Temple was the Mind Temple, which was made entirely of gold. Spiraling pillars stood at the corners, holding up the weight of the roof. There were no engravings or carvings on the gold. Jason felt that it was possibly the most mysterious of the Temples.

Next to the Mind Temple, by a tunnel, was the Storm Temple. The Temple of Lightning. It was made of blue sapphire that shone brilliantly in the sun, sparkling in all directions. Under the roof were engraved clouds that had lightning bolts shooting out of them to the ground. Situated near the entrance were two wolves. Their teeth were bared ferociously and their fur was dark blue with black streaks running through it. The wolves looked so realistic Jason took a step back, almost scared that they might come alive at any moment.

The Temple next to the Storm Temple was the Wind Temple. It was made of pure silver, the same color as thick fog carried in from the ocean by the wind. Tornadoes and hurricanes were drawn on the Temple's smooth surface. The symbol of air was a silver eagle. The eagle flew around the Temple, its feathers bristling with each beat of its wings.

Last, but definitely not least was the Stone Temple. It was made entirely out of stone and marble. Vines ran over it, claiming ownership of the Temple. The vines acted like the Temple's veins. The earth's own energy coursed through the vines, giving life to the Temple. The animal of earth was the badger, a flat-backed creature with black, beady eyes and sharp, menacing teeth.

CHAPTER TEN

"Wow," said Jason in awe.

"It certainly never gets old," said Skylar, running her hand over the marble of the Temple of Prophecies.

"I never thought I would be lucky enough to see them," said the Duchess, hesitantly reaching for the sapphire of the Storm Temple.

Ember rushed into the Flame Temple. She disappeared from sight and Jason knew she probably wouldn't be seen again until lunchtime.

"This is probably the most beautiful thing I have ever seen," said the Duchess, peering into the Stone Temple.

"Wait till you see inside the Water Temple," said Skylar. "Everything inside seems to be made of water."

The Duchess made as if to go inside the Water Temple. But then she shook her head, possibly thinking it would be too much for her. In the end, she just stood there like a statue, her brow furrowed as though she were thinking deeply.

"Shall we get the camp ready then?" asked Morpheus, glancing first at Skylar, then back at the Mind Temple.

"Yes, please Morpheus," said Skylar, leading the Duchess and Jason inside the Water Temple.

Jason took a last glance at Morpheus, but every other thought soon fled his mind at the sight of the Water Temple. The inside of the Temple was much larger than the exterior suggested. The ceiling was so tall and majestic Jason got dizzy from looking upward. The walls of the Temple were made of turquoise just like the outside. But on the wall in front of Jason, and the walls at his sides were waterfalls. They fell from the ceiling into a large pool on the floor that ran across the sides of the Temple from the entrance all around the walls. The waterfalls thundered down into the pool non-stop, yet the pool never overflowed.

"You were right, Skylar," said the Duchess in awe. "The Stone Temple is nothing compared to this."

Skylar smiled, but the smile did not reach her eyes. The water that surrounded her had reminded her of something. Jason could see it in the way she looked at the waterfalls.

"We should go," said Skylar, turning toward the exit. "Morpheus will have lunch almost ready."

The Duchess nodded but stayed in the Temple even after Skylar and Jason had left. Jason looked toward the Flame Temple. He could just imagine Ember in there, marveling at the beauty the Temple held, just as the Duchess had done. He tore his eyes from the Temple, hearing the commotion between Skylar and Morpheus. Morpheus didn't have lunch ready, in fact, he had barely moved from the spot they had left him.

"Morpheus," said Skylar hopelessly, preparing a fire. "I asked you to get lunch ready. What have you been up to?"

"Uh, I just, it just..." muttered Morpheus, without removing his eyes from the Mind Temple.

"Yes, yes. It must have kept you there, that's what," said Skylar, sending sparks flying as she rubbed two stones against each other.

"Sorry, it's just that how did they get that much gold?!" asked Morpheus in a softly exasperated voice. "I mean it's just impossible. I wanted to make the king's chamber out of gold, but appar-

CHAPTER TEN

ently, the miners were all out. Of course, I sued them because they were obviously lying," Morpheus was muttering again.

"Yes, yes. It's just impossible," said Skylar, finally satisfied with the roaring fire in front of her. "But hasn't it entered your mind that the Gifted were very powerful? I wouldn't put it past some of them to make gold, after all, some of them were very talented at alchemy."

"Mm, true, true," said Morpheus.

"Come away from the Temple and help me with lunch, please," said Skylar, starting to become exasperated.

"Oh, alright," said Morpheus, turning away from the Mind Temple.

"Ember!" called Skylar, summoning sandwiches from the castle in the Crystal Kingdom.

Skylar made as if to go towards the Flame Temple when something hit the fireplace, followed by an explosion that rattled the windows of the Temples and threw Skylar backward. Ember ran out of the Flame Temple shouting, but her words were unintelligible. Morpheus ran forward to help Skylar, but his path was cut off as something monstrous stepped in front of him. It was a gigantic black wolf. Its teeth were bared menacingly and its hackles were raised threateningly. Morpheus instinctively summoned his staff and shot a spell at the wolf. The spell bounced off harmlessly. It just agitated the wolf more. The wolf pounced on Morpheus and tried to tear the staff out of his arms.

While this was going on, Ember had joined the fight. She was fighting at Morpheus' side trying to keep more wolves at bay. The wolves were trying to get at Skylar, who had hit her head in the explosion and was now unconscious. Jason was trying to wake her.

"Duchess!" shouted Ember. "If you're hiding, when we're done I'm going to be very angry!"

"Coming," answered the Duchess, running out of the Water Temple and summoning her staff.

The Duchess shot a spell toward a group of wolves running down the mountain. The spell hit the center of the pack, breaking their ranks and setting some of them on fire. The Duchess joining the fight gave new strength to Morpheus. He shot another spell at the wolf that was tackling him. This time the spell hit the wolf square in the face and exploded in its eyes. Ember shot a ball of fire toward the mountain, causing a rock slide.

"You'll kill us all!" said Morpheus, as a ton of debris and rocks started rolling down the hill toward them.

"Not if these wolves kill us first!" said Ember.

Morpheus was conveniently distracted as another wolf pounced on him. The Duchess started shooting spells at the source of the wolves: the entrance to the Temples.

Jason looked at the surrounding chaos. What if he had caused this? What if Skylar was dead because of him? And it would all be just because he was the Keeper. Jason noticed something at the top of the mountain. Was it a giant bird? It looked familiar. Suddenly it hit him. Skylar had described them as fearsome and monstrous beasts. A Shadow Wing had just joined the fight. Onyx was here. Jason stood up and cried out. He knew the real threat was Onyx, not the wolves. He had to try to tell them.

Jason's cry was cut short as something hit him in the shoulder.

CHAPTER TEN

He looked down at his shoulder and was shocked to see an arrow shaft sticking out. A rush of pain made him forget everything else. Jason gasped as he clutched his arm. Blood was pouring down his shoulder and forearm. It hurt like nothing he had ever felt before. He closed his eyes. He felt a numb pain blossom from his shoulder, and felt himself drifting... Someone touched Jason's arm. The pain evaporated for a moment. Jason opened his eyes and looked into Ember's face. Jason looked around him. Onyx had joined the battle. She was fighting Morpheus.

Onyx had a bow slung over her shoulder and a dagger in each hand. Each spell that Morpheus shot missed her. She dodged every attack he aimed at her. Jason looked into her silver eyes. Onyx glanced at him. Jason saw evil in those eyes. Malevolence was written across her features. Onyx delivered a painful blow to Morpheus, stabbing him in the leg. Morpheus fell to his knees. Blood dripped to the floor, the scarlet red liquid staining the bright green grass. Staining earth's core.

Jason felt pain in his heart. The earth was sending a message to his mind. Jason felt new strength flow through him. Earth was letting him control it. Jason stood up and felt the earth with his mind. A vine grew up from the ground and grabbed hold of Onyx. She stabbed at it with her dagger and flew up in the air. Her wing cuffed the Duchess on the head. The Duchess fell to the floor, unconscious.

Onyx rose up in the air and simultaneously grabbed hold of her bow and an arrow. Her bow shot out of her hand as Jason made a vine snatch her wrist. Onyx struggled ferociously and was saved as a fearsome-looking wolf bit the vine and broke it. This wolf looked different from the others. Its fur shone like a million stars and it bared its sharp teeth with savagery. It could have been the blood loss but Jason thought the wolf looked bigger than the others. Much bigger and certainly more threatening.

Jason made an upward motion with his hand; a vine shot up into the air and curled around Onyx's legs. Tighter and tighter. In a single movement, Onyx cut the vine and broke free.

"Enough!" shouted Onyx.

Her shout made everyone freeze. Jason looked around him. Skylar was at his feet, unconscious. Morpheus was on his knees, trying to stop the bleeding. Ember was at Jason's side, grabbing hold of his arm and looking up into Onyx's terrifying face. The Duchess was unconscious and lay in a heap on the floor.

"I do not want to fight," said Onyx, lowering herself to the ground. "I just want the Keeper."

"We'll never give him to you!" said Ember bravely. Jason noticed a cut from her knee to her ankle was bleeding horribly. "He doesn't belong to you."

"He doesn't belong to you either, does he?" said Onyx, a terrible smile playing across her features "Nova?"

Ember flinched at the name, and she suddenly looked vulnerable and lost. Jason grasped her arm and she turned to him. She took a breath, and flickers of red could be seen in her eyes.

"Yes," said Onyx, her silver eyes glinting evilly. "I've studied up on you. After you took Morgana I made it my duty to know everything about you. Especially your real name."

Jason put his hand on Ember's hand when he noticed she was about to do something rash. This was his fight. He had to take care of it.

"You're Onyx, right?" said Jason.

CHAPTER TEN

"That's right," said Onyx. "and you must be the Keeper."

"Yes," said Jason, trying not to show his fear. "I am. Leave us alone."

Onyx laughed, a harsh, malicious sound that echoed throughout the valley.

"I'm afraid I can't leave without you," said Onyx, the laughter still hovering in her eyes. "So if you want me to leave... you'll need to come with me."

"Not a chance," said Ember. Jason noticed flames curling up her wrist. "You'll have to go through me if you want to take him."

"Very well," said Onyx.

"No, Ember," whispered Jason in her ear. "I need to do it."

"It's too dangerous," said Ember quietly. "At least this way I can harm her before she even comes close to you."

"No," said Jason rather harshly. "I won't let you."

"But, Jason–"

Ember's words were lost to Jason as he walked toward Onyx. Jason was ready and tried to hide his fear. Onyx smiled and retrieved her bow. In her eyes was an untameable evil.

Onyx aimed a dagger at Jason. He made a boulder come out of the earth that shielded him from her. Onyx rose up in the air, shooting hundreds of arrows a second. Jason managed to shield himself each time. Jason was blind to the wolf approaching Skylar.

He couldn't look behind him while fighting Onyx. Jason heard a struggle behind him but didn't have time to turn around as Onyx shot another round of arrows at him. Jason gestured upward; a vine burst out of the ground and grabbed hold of Onyx's wing. She called out in pain as she was plucked from the air.

"You'll pay for that, boy," said Onyx as she struggled to her feet.

Jason grew more vines and had them seize Onyx. They curled around her waist, slowly tightening.

"Alright!" said Onyx helplessly. "I will leave."

Jason loosened the vines a bit but kept them around her. He couldn't trust her, at least not completely.

"All right," said Jason. "If I let you go, will you leave with the wolves?"

"Of course," said Onyx, an evil glint appearing in her eyes for a second.

"Okay then," said Jason.

Claws tore into Jason's back and he felt a wolf hit him in the head. He felt a slashing pain go through his leg and fell to the floor. The vines around Onyx let go as Jason lost his connection with the earth.

"Thank you, Keeper," said Onyx, stepping over Jason. "I will be taking this woman as prisoner. To rescue her you must go to the Phoenix Mountains. Call for a raven. It will lead you the rest of the way. This isn't exactly what Invictius wanted, but I'd like to give you a choice. It's much more entertaining. Meet us at the mountains before the full moon and I will exchange this woman for you. Otherwise, she dies."

Jason heard the dragging of a body and the soft paw steps of hundreds of wolves. Jason reluctantly and slowly drifted off into unconsciousness. The last thing he heard was the beating of Onyx's wings.

the Keeper of the Elements

CHAPTER ELEVEN

Family

"Jason, Jason."

Ember shook Jason till he awoke. His head hurt and the events of the day before came back to him in a rush of emotion. As usual, Ember was waking him up. Jason saw in her eyes that there was something wrong, that she was terribly worried and upset.

"What happened?" asked Jason, rubbing his head with a grimace.

"Skylar's been kidnapped," said Ember, the sentence rolling off her tongue like a single word. "Onyx took her."

It all came back to him. The beat of Onyx's wings still echoed in his ears.

"It is not your fault," said Morpheus, his face hidden in the shadows cast by the Temples. "We could barely protect you and now Onyx has gone and kidnapped Skylar."

Jason couldn't believe it. He had been fighting Onyx and he had failed. It was his fault, no matter what Morpheus said. Jason sat up shakily and looked around. He could see Morpheus' flowing robes disappearing into the shadows. The Duchess was holding ice to her head and groaning quietly. And of course, there was Ember, sitting beside him with a torn expression on her face and making images in the fire.

"How did Onyx take her?" asked Jason, determined to get the full story.

"A wolf attacked me while you and Onyx were fighting," said Ember, as the fire morphed into vivid images that illustrated her story. "He managed to overpower me with the help of some other wolves. They forced me to stay down and I had to watch as a wolf hit you in the head, allowing Onyx to take Skylar. By the time I managed to fight him off, Onyx had already left the Temples."

"So technically," said the Duchess. "It's her fault."

"Duchess," said Morpheus threateningly.

"Fine," said the Duchess. "But Skylar would still be here if Ember could have gotten rid of those wolves."

"It doesn't matter," said Jason. "Onyx could have captured any one of us. Right now I don't care whose fault it is. Right now I want to know when the full moon is."

"In three days," said Morpheus. "But what use is that knowledge?"

"Because he wants to rescue Skylar," said Ember, standing up as the realization hit her. "You can't do that, Jason! Onyx will take you instead."

"No," said Jason, "she won't. Because we're going to sneak in and rescue her. Onyx said to find a raven near the Phoenix

CHAPTER ELEVEN

Mountains. Morpheus, do you know where Invictius might be with that information?"

"Well," said Morpheus hesitantly. "There's supposed to be a hidden castle in those mountains. But it's been abandoned for years."

"Are you sure about this, Jason?" asked Ember.

Jason hesitated, but not for long. Skylar had taken him in when his mother had died. She had educated and protected him. It was Jason's turn to protect her now.

"I am,' said Jason.

"All right, then that castle is our best shot," said Ember, deciding to help Jason despite it going against her instincts.

"All right, then it's decided," said Jason.

"It's not decided," said the Duchess. "Skylar would want you to go into hiding, and she'd want you to be safe. Doing this is going against her wishes."

"How do you know?" asked Morpheus. "Skylar would want Jason to do what he thinks is right, and I learned about all the entrances to the castle during the Third World War. I think we have a pretty good chance."

"I know Skylar would not want this," said the Duchess. "She cares more about Jason than herself."

"True," said Ember. "But she also loves Jason enough to trust him and let him do what he thinks is best."

The Duchess looked at Morpheus. But he seemed determined to support Jason's decision. Ember appeared even more so.

"Fine," said the Duchess in exasperation. "I give up. Let's go."

"Yes!" said Jason. "I mean, thank you."

The Duchess said nothing.

"Can you bring us there, Morpheus?" asked Jason.

"Yes, I've been there once before. But I warn you, Invictius has probably been living there a while, so he will know the secret passages too."

"Okay, when we get there you can tell us which ones you know," said Jason.

"All right," said Morpheus, summoning his staff. "Ready, prepare yourselves!"

Jason closed his eyes, fully aware of what would come next. When he next opened them they were at the mountains. A vast landscape of steep hills and gigantic mountains awaited him when he opened his eyes. But Morpheus and Ember were also waiting for him. Morpheus led them up the mountain in single file. The Duchess was last and made a blue fur coat appear around her. Jason thought longingly of how warm it would be if he had a coat like that.

After only a few minutes they reached a cave. Morpheus lowered his pack on the ground and sat in a far corner. The rest of the group followed his example.

"All right," began Morpheus, as if he was about to tell a story.

CHAPTER ELEVEN

"One of the entrances is right here. There are tunnels starting from here that run inside the mountain leading to the castle. Another entrance is magical, but requires a password that can be changed from inside the castle. So I don't think we'll manage to get in that way. The last way I know of is the top of the mountain. If you blast it then it will open like a trap door."

"Which do you think we should go through?" asked Jason.

"I think the first one is the best actually," said Morpheus. "It goes right to the dungeons which are rarely guarded because it's almost impossible to escape from the cells. Plus, they wouldn't expect anyone to be trying to get deeper into the castle and Skylar's probably being held there."

"All right," said Jason. "Who agrees to go this way?"

"The dungeons?" asked the Duchess, shivering in disgust. "They stink. I'd never go to a filthy place like that."

"Well that's too bad," said Ember. "We're going to save Skylar and you're coming with us."

"Fine," said the Duchess. "But I'm not going anywhere near the prisoners."

"Whatever," said Ember.

"All right," said Jason. "So the plan is we go into the dungeons, find Skylar, and come back here."

"What if Skylar's not in the dungeons?" asked the Duchess.

"Then we search the rest of the castle," said Jason. "But we can't completely split up. Ember will come with me and Morpheus will stay with you."

"Are you sure Ember will manage to protect you?" asked Morpheus. "She isn't exactly the most trustworthy person."

"It was one time!" said Ember in anger.

"Two," said Morpheus. "You stole the dragon egg and the king's staff. I had every reason to send the Warlocks after you."

"No, you didn't! I only stole the egg to save Skylar's life and the staff was because you wouldn't listen to me and it was the only thing to stop the war."

"I didn't listen to you because you stole the egg!"

"Enough!" said Jason, his anger manifesting physically as the earth started shaking. "I can't have you two fighting all the time. This is why I put you with the Duchess, Morpheus."

Morpheus seemed taken aback but said nothing. He just glared at Ember, who returned the look of hatred passionately.

"Now, do you remember the plan?" said Jason.

They nodded. Morpheus and Ember didn't look away from each other. The Duchess didn't seem to think it was much of a plan though, and made a point of repeating this while making it clear she wasn't listening.

"Let's go," said Jason.

Morpheus lit the gem of his staff up and Ember set her arms on fire. With their light to guide them, they all headed inside.

CHAPTER ELEVEN

The going was rough and tiring and though the tunnel was man-made it had clearly been done in a hurry. Rocks littered the stone ground, and the walls were rugged and uneven. Jason stumbled more than once and soon got very annoyed with the ground. He unconsciously started shaping the walls and ground by using the earth and was surprised when he noticed that the stone ground was suddenly much smoother.

The Duchess had noticed the change and looked suspiciously at Jason. She shrugged her shoulders when she noticed Ember looking at her.

Ember noticed a light and a corner ahead and slowed down, dimming her blazing arms. She put her finger over her lips as a signal to the others. Soon they were all creeping toward the light. Jason came to the corner and hesitated. The Duchess went on ahead instead. They came out in a long underground corridor. The light they had seen was coming from a torch attached to a wall.

The Duchess kept on walking, stopping whenever she heard a sound, but more than once it was just a small rock falling from the ceiling.

Soon there was more noise than just that of falling rocks. There was the sound of the jangling of chains or the rattling of metal bars. The Duchess slowed down and Ember went on ahead. She stopped at a corner, possibly because she had spotted a guard. After what seemed an eternity she signaled to the others and crept out of sight.

The sight that met Jason's eyes depicted a sad and terrible fate. Hundreds of prisoners sat in cells that stank of dampness and mold. Their eyes were lost and hopeless. They looked even worse than the prisoners in the Crystal Castle.

One prisoner that caught Jason's eye didn't look like the others. The prisoner was a girl who looked about two years older than Jason. Her hair was blacker than a raven's feathers and cut at chin length, accentuating her cheek bones. Her eyes were a mystical sea green. There was something in her face that was different from the other prisoner's. Their eyes were dead and didn't have a spark of hope in them. But hers were still alive. As if she knew that someday, no matter how far in the future, someone would save her. As if she knew that someday Invictius would encounter the fate he deserved.

The girl looked up as Jason's shadow fell on her face. She noticed the Duchess and Morpheus standing behind him as well as Ember's outline in the shadows.

"Who are you?" asked the girl, for a split second a sliver of mistrust showing in her sea green eyes.

"I'm Jason. We're here to rescue my aunt," said Jason, instantly sensing her mistrust.

"Jason," said Ember sharply. "You shouldn't trust any of these people. They could be tricking you. Invictius could have found out you were coming and planted a traitor here, hoping you would free him... or her."

"Please!" whispered the girl. "I am a real prisoner here. Invictius captured me a few years ago. He killed my family!"

Jason thought for a moment. And as he looked around he wished he could save every single one of the prisoners –but he knew that was impossible. But even one prisoner could make a difference. One prisoner could possibly destroy Invictius' plans. He couldn't care less what Ember said at this moment. He would help this girl escape.

CHAPTER ELEVEN

"Cast a spell to unlock the cell," said Jason to Morpheus.

"Are you crazy?" whispered Ember in Jason's ear. "Invictius is smarter than he seems, he could have known Onyx wouldn't capture you and planned ahead. Besides, it would be easy to come up with the story that Invictius killed her family."

"I trust her," answered Jason simply.

Morpheus cast a spell on the lock, there was a click and the door swung open. The girl stepped out of the cell and shot Ember a mistrustful look.

"Thank you," said the girl to Jason. "My name is Diana."

"Mine's Jason," said Jason, shaking her hand.

"Now is no time for formalities," said Morpheus urgently. "We must hurry. Search for Skylar."

They spread out. Diana followed Jason and avoided Ember's accusing eyes. Jason couldn't find Skylar and soon started blaming himself for Skylar's capture.

"She doesn't seem to be here," said the Duchess, who made a point of avoiding Diana, probably because of the odor emanating from her.

"We need to search the rest of the castle," said Morpheus in a whisper. "Come this way."

He led them through a series of dark and damp corridors. After a few minutes they came to an intersection.

"This is where we split up," said the Duchess.

"Okay," said Jason. "Good luck. Diana, who do you want to go with?"

"Whom are you going with?" asked Diana.

"Ember. She'll be accompanying me,"

"Wait, Jason," said Morpheus, worry showing in his blue eyes. "Are you sure Ember can protect you and Diana?"

"I know how to protect myself," said Diana quietly. "I'm a Gifted."

The Duchess gasped and seemed to almost faint. The others looked at Diana in surprise. Ember looked frustrated, untrusting.

"You share the Gifted power?!" whispered Ember in anger. "I can't believe it! If you're tricking us, you're going to regret it."

"I rather doubt that," said Diana.

"What's that supposed to mean?!" said Ember, scarlet fire glowing in her eyes.

"Shh," said Morpheus urgently.

Ember immediately fell silent, but she looked at Diana with a face full of mistrust. A shadow fell upon the wall opposite Jason. It obviously belonged to a guard, but soon it walked away. Jason sighed in relief. Morpheus nodded to Jason as if to say goodbye, then he and the Duchess took the branch to the right. Ember glanced after them before leading the way on the left.

It was easier to walk here than the entrance. The workers that had molded this tunnel out of the mountain had paid careful

CHAPTER ELEVEN

attention to detail. Jason didn't need to think about rocks or crevices, instead, his mind was free to wander among the questions he had for Diana. He didn't think now was the right time to ask his many questions though. Perhaps if they got out of here he would have time.

"Stop," said Ember, quietly but urgently.

The light of a torch wavered on the wall in front of them. The torch that emitted the light was just out of sight, behind the corner. But a dark shadow blocked out most of the light. Someone seemed to be waiting for them.

"I'll go first," mouthed Jason to Ember.

She shook her head, then pointed first to herself, then to Jason. Jason pointed to Diana and shrugged his shoulders, hoping Ember would understand. Diana half groaned, half sighed and walked past Jason. Ember tried to stop her; after a short struggle Diana walked past her and out of sight. Jason heard a loud splash and a soft thump. The tall shadow that had been cast on the wall had been replaced by a shorter and smaller shadow. Ember grabbed Jason's wrist and practically dragged him to Diana. The unconscious body of a soldier lay on the floor. He looked as if he had been dunked in the sea.

"What were you thinking?" asked Ember, fury etched into the hazel of her eyes. "Are you crazy?! That guard could have hurt you or something!"

"Do you trust me now?" asked Diana, as if she hadn't heard a word Ember had said.

"Trust you?" exploded Ember. "You're crazy! You could have exposed us."

"No," said Diana quite breezily. "He was probably just a young trainee. Invictius is training thousands of soldiers as if he's expecting more battles."

"Soldiers?" asked Ember in shocked surprise.

"Yep," said Diana. "Watch it."

Diana casually flicked her wrist. Water appeared out of thin air and surrounded another guard, encircling him into a levitating ball of water. Ember turned in surprise and her jaw dropped to resemble the gaping mouth of a fish. She closed it, looking irritated, and continued leading Jason and Diana through the dim corridor.

"Not even a thank you?" said Diana, following the infuriated figure of Ember. "No? Nothing?"

Ember just groaned and walked on in silence. Jason shrugged his shoulders at Diana and continued to follow Ember. He heard Diana sigh behind him.

The corridors were brighter in this part of the underground castle. More torches had been secured to the stone walls, casting light on those who walked beneath them. Here there were also windows. Ember ducked whenever they approached one.

Instead of endless corridors or cells, there were rooms. Some rooms were separated from the corridors by actual doors. Others —the more dangerous of the two— were just arched entryways. Ember would stop wherever they approached one of these entrances and make sure there was no-one inside, and once she was sure, she would continue on her way. Diana would get impatient and would start leading the way when Ember did this. So more than once a small argument would erupt between the two warrior-spirited Gifted.

Jason tried to split them up wherever this happened, but he soon found out that if he did this they would both round on him for interrupting them. On one of these occasions, Jason forced both of them in a room because he had heard the most dreaded sound possible. Footsteps.

Ember fell on her back as Jason pushed her in the room and Diana stumbled backward. Jason looked behind him and realized his mistake too late. The light from the corridors spilled through the arched doorway and into the room. The guard that was slowly walking toward them would instantly notice them if he looked inside.

Ember had heard the reason why Jason had pushed her inside and was no longer looking at him like she would like to strangle him. Diana too, was sitting absolutely still, waiting for the moment when she would be exposed and thrown back into the dungeons.

A shadow fell on the floor of the room. Jason stepped into the surrounding shadows out of fright. Whatever kind of guard this was, it was badly misshapen. The shadow looked more like a creature than anything. A creature with a long neck, spines running down its back and large terrifying wings.

"Xander," said a drawling, wheezy voice just out of sight. "The master wants you."

"In which room, servant?" asked the owner of the shadow, the dragon.

"In the throne room. He said that he demanded your presence immediately and that Onyx is there with a prisoner."

"I will be there," said Xander, his deep, growling voice resonating throughout the corridor.

Soft, quick footsteps hurried away. And as Xander walked through the corridor and behind a corner, the heavy, scraping sound his footsteps made almost forced Jason to cover his ears.

Diana looked at the dragon's retreating shadow with hatred, hatred that was obviously directed toward Invictius. Jason felt his face getting hot, for Ember's face was filled with dread and Jason could actually feel the energy building up in her hands, an obvious sign that she was enraged at what the servant had called Skylar. Prisoner. They had her in the throne room at that very moment.

Jason silently started following the dragon, leading Ember and Diana. After a moment, Ember and Diana followed him. Jason crept on ahead wherever he got the chance, and before long he heard the dragon's screeching footsteps stop and the creaking sound of doors opening.

"Enter," said a voice. A voice that somehow held so much loathing and darkness that it made Jason recoil.

The dragon entered the room and the doors started to slowly close. Jason barely had time to creep inside without being seen. There was no light in the room except the silvery moonlight filtering in from a high window, so it was reasonably easy for Jason to sneak into a corner without being seen. Jason allowed his eyes to adjust to the dimness of the room, and was quietly amazed at what he saw. A throne made of silver stood pushed up against a wall. The moonlight that entered the room made it sparkle majestically. Jason looked up as a noise caught his ears and he noticed a large raven perched on one of the rafters. But his attention was diverted again as the dragon spoke.

CHAPTER ELEVEN

"You called for me, Lord Invictius," said the dragon, bowing his scaly, horned head to no-one in particular.

"Yes, I did, Xander," said a man, suddenly appearing out of the shadows. "We have a matter of importance to discuss. It seems Onyx found where the boy was hiding."

The ghastly Onyx stepped out of a corner. Her elegant head was raised with a selfish pride encircling her like a crown. Jason noticed her horrifying black feathered wings were spread wide in defiance.

"She has brought us her catch," said Invictius, reposing himself on the throne. "The boy's aunt, it seems."

Skylar was pushed out of a corner by two gruesome looking guards. Jason barely recognized her. Her cloak was ripped and her hair was a mess. She had cuts all over her arms and horrible bruises on her wrists that could barely be seen under the chains holding them. Dry blood was caked in a sticky mess on one side of her face. At beholding this sight, Jason had a desperate urge to kill Onyx for what she had done. Jason prepared himself to jump out of his corner, but a warm hand caught his wrist. He looked into Ember's face, her anger apparent in her scarlet colored eyes, but there was also patience there. She was waiting for the right moment to attack.

"Onyx," continued Invictius, his soft voice emanating hatred with each word, "against my orders, has not captured the boy. Instead, she decided to have a little fun and take this woman. Of course, I have nothing against breaking the boy's heart in two, but this is not what I asked for."

"I thought you would enjoy a little fun, Invictius," said Onyx.

"She can spend some time with the Gifted you have in the dungeons."

"Gifted?" asked Xander. "We have a Gifted?"

"Morgana captured her," said Onyx. "The Gifted's been rotting in there for about three years. I've told Invictius to take care of her before it was too late. She has spirit, and I am sure she will escape before long."

"I already told you that we have been conducting experiments on her," said Invictius. Jason noticed Diana flinch. "We have been attempting to separate her from her power. Unfortunately, the incompetent scientists you captured from Futura are useless. They know nothing of magic and keep getting themselves killed. But, however enjoyable it is to talk about how we torture the Gifted, I did not send for Xander to talk about this. Instead, we must put up defenses for the boy."

"Defenses?" laughed Xander. "He is just a boy, my lord. I am sure he won't even manage to find this place."

"That is why you are not in charge of making the plans. You are a foolish dragon, Xander. You forget that this is not a normal boy. He is a Gifted and the Keeper. He will have mastered one of the original elements by now. And we are all doomed if it is earth. But what I want from you, Xander, is to put up defenses."

"Surely–"

"Xander!" said Invictius menacingly. "Put up the defenses, or I assure you, you will be next in line for the experiments."

"Yes, my lord," said Xander, cowardice etched in his eyes.

CHAPTER ELEVEN

Xander bowed and retreated from the room. Jason heard him growl as the doors clanged shut. Onyx folded her wings and took hold of Skylar's wrist. Skylar whimpered in pain as Onyx's long fingernails dug into her flesh.

"What do I do with this filth?" asked Onyx, practically lifting Skylar off the floor.

"Leave her here," said Invictius. "I will question her on what she knows about her dear nephew."

Jason noticed a small smile pass over Onyx's face. There was no doubt at all that Onyx was cruel.

"Leave now," said Invictius, standing up. "Leave us."

"Yes, my lord," said Onyx, obviously relieved to be dismissed.

Onyx let go of Skylar without the smallest thought for her. Unlike Xander, she didn't bow to Invictius, instead leaving the room without a word.

"Now," said Invictius softly. "I have been looking for the boy for years. Finally I have something he loves. Tell me, Skylar, does he know?"

Jason's brow furrowed as he thought of what Invictius had said. Was he still talking about him? Or had he moved on to another subject?

"I used to trust you, Vic!" said Skylar in desperate fury. "You used to be my best friend!"

Jason gasped but closed his mouth again. Best friend? Invictius had been Skylar's best friend? Jason trembled with the effort he used to stop himself from running at Skylar to demand the truth. The questions that sprang to his mind made his heart race.

"Yes," said Invictius. "I was, wasn't I? But that is not what I want to know. Does the boy know?"

Skylar refused to speak. Her eyes were focused on the outside world, and her gaze did not shift away from the window.

"Dear Skylar," tutted Invictius impatiently. "I know you wish to tell me. You still have that same look you used to have when we were friends. I know you still have feelings for me."

Skylar looked away from him, her jaw clenched.

"All right, if that is your wish," said Invictius. There was no kindness in his voice.

In one motion Invictius made his staff appear. It was made of ebony, with silver tracings inside it. The orb suspended between the interlaced branches was black, like Invictius' heart and soul.

"I do not want to torture you, Skylar. All I want to know is if he knows."

Skylar looked up at him defiantly. She did not speak, but the words she wished to say were expressed in her eyes. Invictius raised his staff, the orb directed toward Skylar's face.

"No!"

Ember shot out of nowhere and grabbed hold of Invictius' staff. An expression of shock and surprise took hold of Invictius' emotions for a second, but just as quickly his face was wiped of emotion as he fought off Ember with little more than the smallest effort.

"Ember!" said Skylar, standing up shakily.

Diana hurried to help Skylar up and Jason stepped out of the shadows. The surprise and fear in Skylar's face was unmistakable as she looked at him. But she soon turned away as Diana led her out of the room and out of danger. Jason summoned the earth to do his bidding, and forced the mountain to start crumbling where Invictius stood. Unfortunately, Jason's plan had a flaw, and soon the whole mountain started crumbling uncontrollably.

"Get out of here!" ordered Ember, as she finally broke free from Invictius' grasp. "Hurry!"

Jason ran out of the throne room, the urgency in Ember's voice making it evident that she didn't want or need help. Jason ran into Skylar, who was trying to return to the room even though Diana was clinging onto her arm.

"Jason!" said Skylar in relief, drawing him toward her with a hug. "You shouldn't have come."

"We need to go!" said Ember, running toward them. "The whole mountain top is going to collapse!"

Jason withdrew from Skylar and grabbed her wrist. Together they started running toward the closest exit possible. Diana led them through so many corridors that Jason lost count. Everywhere there was chaos. Guards were trying to escape, desperate to get out of the way of falling boulders. Finally, Diana led them into a room that had somehow been left untouched. Ember came in soon after them and almost fell to the floor, panting.

"What happened?" asked Diana, gasping for breath.

"Jason..." said Ember, wheezing. "Jason... controlled... earth."

"Really?" said Diana, willing for a bit more breath to enter her lungs. "That's... great!"

Ember laughed but immediately went into a coughing fit. Skylar smiled at Jason and summoned her staff. And though she looked worn out and was no-doubt exhausted, Jason still saw a fire in her eyes that he was glad to see.

"We should get going," said Skylar.

"You're right," said Ember, standing up with a bit of effort. "We should really get going. Invictius seemed angry, and I have no doubt he'll come chasing after us if we don't leave his beloved castle."

Diana laughed.

"Let's go," said Skylar, making as if to leave the temporary safety of the room.

"Not so fast," said a terribly familiar voice.

Out of the shadows of the room came a dignified looking lady with furs covering her feeble neck. The Duchess, for that was who the lady was, finally revealing her true self.

"Luna?" said Skylar, fear flashing in her eyes. "No! No, Luna!"

"Ah, I see my master told you about my deeds," said the Duchess, her malicious smile revealing her snow-white teeth. "I am happy you know. I am happy you now know that I wanted your family

CHAPTER ELEVEN

torn apart. I have been serving Lord Invictius for a dreadfully long time; he approached me one day, and I was hesitant to meet him, but after a cup of tea it all became clear to me; Amethyst had to go, you had to go. I have been following his orders ever since the Third World War. I was a spy, a traitor. As a noble-lady I was immediately forgiven for the death of your sister. I gave that information to Invictius on purpose, hoping he would kill your sister. I hated you, detested you. I hoped my master would kill you too. But then I realized that having your heart torn in two would be enough. It would be enough if you thought your best friend had betrayed you and if your sister was dead. It would be enough to see the horrified expression on your face when my lord kills the only family you have left: Jason."

The Duchess' pale face turned toward Jason. Her lips curled upward when she met his eyes.

"Oh, Jason," said the Duchess softly. "I watched your dear Skylar crumble when your mother died. I saw how hurt she was, and now I can't wait to see her face when you die. Killed by the hand of my great master."

Ember tried to shoot forward, but she was stopped by Diana, who was keeping a hold on Ember's cloak. Ember drew back, but the signs of hatred were still etched on her face. The Duchess laughed at Ember's attempt to hurt her. The Duchess' laughter carried across the room, an evil laughter woven out of cold hatred.

"Where is Morpheus?" demanded Ember.

Jason was surprised. After the weeks of traveling they had done, Ember hadn't shown any love to Morpheus. Even the Duchess seemed taken aback.

"You want to know where Morpheus is?" said the Duchess, her smile growing wider. "Oh, I had to force him down like a filthy dog, and I am afraid that he has been terribly hurt."

The Duchess summoned her staff and summoned Morpheus from some unknown place. Morpheus appeared on the floor. His eyes were closed, and his limp body looked forlorn without his staff.

"If you killed him you're going to pay for it!" said Ember.

The Duchess laughed.

"Don't worry little girl, he's not dead, just… just temporarily useless. Not that he was any different when he was awake."

"How could you do this, Luna?" said Skylar. The Duchess flinched when she used her name. "We were best friends! You were like family!"

"We were never friends, I realize that now. When my master kills Jason, I plan to kill you. Until then, I will have to settle on the death of your beloved student."

The Duchess turned to Ember. In one quick motion the Duchess' staff disappeared, allowing cold ice to erupt from her fingertips. The ice was directed toward Ember's heart, but it never got there. In one movement Jason threw up his arm, willing the earth to hand him a boulder. A tall, piercing rock shot out of the ground. The Duchess' ice hit it and the rock froze over.

"You're the Gifted of ice?" asked Skylar in disbelief.

The Duchess ignored Skylar, her fury increased by Jason's simple act. She rounded on him with anger and madness in her eyes.

CHAPTER ELEVEN

The room started freezing over, the ice feeding on the Duchess' evil heart. The ice started at the ceiling and slowly spread down the walls. With every passing second, it came closer to Jason and everyone in the room.

"Now you will find out how it feels to have a frozen heart," laughed the Duchess happily.

"No," said Jason more bravely than he felt. "We won't."

Jason gestured his hand downward. After a moment of resistance the ceiling started crumbling and the roof started falling in. Ember shot a ball of fire in the Duchess' direction and rushed towards Morpheus while the Duchess dodged the hurtling flames. Ember dragged Morpheus towards Skylar with Diana's help. Jason turned and caught Skylar's hand. Together they ran toward Ember, Diana and Morpheus. When they were near enough, Ember took Jason's hand.

A moment before Jason was teleported, the Duchess emitted a furious, terrible scream as a piercing rock fell down on her. Jason closed his eyes and felt himself being sucked out of the mountains. To safety. To refuge. And hopefully not to the Sacred Temples of the Ancient.

the Keeper of the Elements

CHAPTER TWELVE

The Truth

Jason stirred in his sleep. Vivid flashes of his memories caused restless dreams. He saw the Duchess, her arms outstretched over a sea of ice, hatred and fear in her eyes.

The dream changed. He saw Skylar in chains. Alone and hurt. This memory pained Jason, and he mumbled in his sleep as the dream changed again.

There was Onyx, flying over the field beside the Sacred Temples. Her black feathered wings opened threateningly. Her laughter echoed in Jason's mind.

The dream returned to Skylar. The expression on her face was sad as she looked around the Water Temple. Loss could be seen in her eyes. Loss and pain.

As the scene faded away, the dream changed. There was Invictius. In the dream Jason had time to study him properly. Invictius had black and evil eyes. Even the way his hands gripped his staff seemed cruel. Half of Invictius' face was hidden in the shadow of his cloak that billowed around Invictius as if it had life of its own. Jason watched from nearby. In the dream he could control himself, and Jason used this freedom to walk toward Invictius.

Invictius looked up as Jason approached him. A passionate hatred appeared in Invictius' eyes.

"Do you know?" Invictius asked Jason.

"Know what?" asked Jason in turn, surprised by how calm he felt. But he knew in real life he would be scared witless.

"You will know," said Invictius, as he started slowly fading away. "In time, you will know."

Invictius disappeared, the dust he was made of falling away completely. Jason turned to look behind him. He saw a beautiful field with the red sun setting under the mountains. He only had a second to take in this beautiful sight. Jason soon heard a voice calling him, and his consciousness snapped back to reality.

"Jason?" said Ember, who was kneeling down next to him. "Are you all right?"

"Yes," mumbled Jason softly with his eyes still closed. "I'm good. Why?"

"You were muttering in your sleep," said Skylar, who was sitting a little distance away. "We were worried."

"I'm good," said Jason, though his heart beat wildly in his chest as he thought of what Invictius had said.

"Go back to sleep then," said Skylar, her head dropping back onto her pillow.

Ember glanced at Jason but shuffled back to her own bed, a makeshift pile of leaves that was not for those accustomed to luxury. Jason opened his eyes and quietly watched Ember turn her

CHAPTER TWELVE

back on him as she also attempted to succumb to the dreamworld. Jason couldn't return to sleep, he couldn't enter the mysterious world of his dreams with these recent visions in his mind. As silently as possible, Jason slipped out of his own leafy bed and left the cave they had found temporary refuge in.

He made his way out of the cave with ease he had no idea he possessed. Outside, the sun had not yet risen. The stars still twinkled brightly as they shed their light on the world below. Jason looked around to assure himself that no creature was near. Reassured, Jason found a comfortable niche in which to seat himself.

Jason found himself thinking about the Duchess. About that night that seemed to have happened years ago. In truth, it had just been a week ago. Ember had managed to transport them to a cave she remembered camping in when Morpheus had set the entire Kingdom against her. They had transported seconds before the whole mountain had fallen in. The cave Ember had found was comfortable enough, and for some reason they hadn't left it ever since they had barely escaped the Duchess. Jason had reason to believe that this was mostly because of Skylar and Diana. He had noticed that they had talked a lot over the past week, but they had tried to keep their discussions secret from Jason, and even more suspiciously, Ember. Jason had no idea what their conversations consisted of, but somehow it didn't seem to matter.

Jason's mind turned back to Invictius. To Invictius' emotionless face. An expressionless face that was undoubtedly the last image many people saw before being sent to the next world. Jason sighed in annoyance. He couldn't have this bothering him anymore. He had to find out what Invictius was talking about. What did Jason need to know?

Was Invictius even talking about Jason? How did Skylar and Invictius know each other? How had they been best friends?

These thoughts and questions troubled Jason more than he could understand. Jason thought he wouldn't manage to sleep for the rest of the night, but soon he was drifting back to his dreams. Dreams that took hold of him and carried him away. Into nothingness. And beyond.

* * *

"Where's Jason?" asked Skylar, the question resounding within the cave and out into the forest.

"Jason!" called Ember.

Jason heard their voices and his eyes fluttered open.

"I'm here," said Jason, as he clambered down from the side of the hill.

Diana and Skylar came out of the cave, and Jason heard Skylar breathe a sigh of relief.

"Are you ok? Why are you out here?" asked Diana.

Jason glanced at her and sighed.

"Skylar," said Jason. "I need to talk to you."

Skylar seemed taken aback, and something akin to fear appeared in her eyes. Jason noticed Diana glance at Skylar, but Jason did not dwell on this. He had to speak to Skylar.

"All right, Jason," said Skylar. "But let's have breakfast first."

Breakfast was a quiet affair, the only noises being the clinking of cutlery on plates and the cheery whistling of the birds outside.

CHAPTER TWELVE

Jason was impatient to get it over with as fast as possible. The question that had disturbed his dreams was the only thought to occupy his mind. Unfortunately, he would have to wait longer than he thought.

Ember had sent word to Lucinda of their whereabouts using Morpheus as a messenger, who had returned to the king's side and wasn't too happy about being assigned this 'trivial responsibility', as he put it. The cleaning up of the morning meal was interrupted as a familiar figure came walking amidst the towering trees. Ember hurried out to greet Lucinda the second she had seen her silhouette. Within minutes, Lucinda was hugging Skylar and Ember and smiling in Jason's direction..

"So Morpheus found you?" asked Ember, who seemed determined to make sure Morpheus had obeyed her request.

"Yes," laughed Lucinda, her smile growing wider. "He found me in the kitchens, and he looked furious. It took a few tries for him to tell me what you wanted because he couldn't get the words out."

Ember laughed for the first time since the incident with the Duchess. It seemed light and cheerful, completely opposite to what Jason was feeling.

With the silence taking over, Lucinda tried to break it by introducing herself to Diana. Diana barely acknowledged Lucinda's presence, so it wasn't a very warm greeting for a first impression. Lucinda withdrew her welcoming hand from Diana's lost gaze, and quickly distracted herself from Diana's sad figure by talking animatedly with Ember about the various events at the castle. According to Lucinda, the king had gotten deathly sick, that being the reason behind Morpheus' departure.

This seemed to shock Skylar, who hadn't been told anything by Morpheus, so she made herself busy cleaning the small cave as a means to distract herself. Noting this, Lucinda and Ember moved their gossiping outside, where their voices could barely be heard.

Jason thought, with that distraction gone, he could finally talk to Skylar. But she avoided him. Whenever he opened his mouth to speak, she would turn away or make an excuse. Diana seemed distressed by this.

"Skylar, please," said Jason, exasperated. "I need to ask you something."

"I'm sorry, Jason," said Skylar, without looking up. "Not now. I... I– I'm busy."

"Please," said Jason, at his wit's end. "It's urgent."

Skylar opened her mouth to make another excuse, but her stuttering was immediately silenced by a few well-chosen words.

"He needs to know," said Diana.

Skylar sighed. She knew when she was beaten. Diana looked expectantly at Skylar and Jason felt a rush of gratitutde toward Diana.

"All right," said Skylar, sitting down on a rock. "Tell me what it is."

"Do you promise you will tell the truth?" asked Jason seriously.

"I promise I will tell the truth, the whole truth and nothing but the truth," said Skylar, a faint smile upon her lips.

CHAPTER TWELVE

Reassured, Jason began, "Why did Invictius say you were best friends?"

"Because we were," said Skylar simply, though for a second her expression changed as if she had expected Jason to ask a different question.

"How?" said Jason. "I mean, how did you meet?"

Skylar sighed again. The sadness and pain in her eyes threatened to overwhelm Jason's heart, but he didn't know why.

"We met in the Third World War. We were both Warlocks, meaning we were both Wizard soldiers. We were instantly best friends, because we were so alike... at least that's what I thought. The first few battles we fought won victory for the rebellion of the Crystal Kingdom. Invictius and I were supporters of the rebellion and our army awarded a name for itself; the Rebels. The war was between three armies. In the army of the Crystal Kingdom was Morpheus, who was my enemy at the time. In the Rebel's army there were me, Invictius, the Duchess and Ember. Finally, the army of the Invaders was fighting to take power for themselves, unlike us, who were fighting to give the power back to the people. We thought the government of the Kingdom was corrupt and unfair. So we struck out against it." Skylar paused and sighed again. In her eyes Jason could see the pain this explanation was costing her.

"In one of the last battles of the Third World War," began Skylar again. "Invictius was wounded in battle. I stood with him the whole time, protecting him from the soldiers of the other armies. In the midst of the battle, though, I turned my back to fight an enemy soldier. In that second I didn't keep an eye on Invictius he disappeared. I never found him again... until the ultimate battle of the Third World War. He was on the Invaders' side.

As a Gifted he offered a huge advantage to the Invaders. They had been losing... now they started winning. He seemed more powerful, and at his hand both the Rebels and the Kingdom's supporters together were almost crushed. When all hope seemed lost, the two defeated armies joined sides. And with the force of a million Wizards, we managed to defeat Invictius. After the war I had time to dwell upon this. And my heart broke because of what Invictius had done."

The enchantment Skylar had cast upon Jason with her narration broke, but his enraptured gaze remained transfixed on Skylar's face. Jason didn't know if it was due to wonder or shock. Out of the corner of his eyes Jason saw Diana looking at Skylar too. The story had captured her attention as well. Skylar had tears gathering in her eyes, and she shook her head but didn't brush them away.

"You have more to say," said Diana, tearing her eyes away from Skylar and into Jason's puzzled eyes.

"Yes," said Skylar calmly, turning to him. "Yes, I do. Jason, I have kept this from you your whole life. I actually don't know how to say this, and I hope you will forgive me. I'm sorry I kept this from you, but I had no idea what to do, and I was ashamed of the truth."

"Skylar," said Jason, gathering her hand in his, in what he hoped was a comforting way. "Just tell me. I won't be angry, I promise."

Skylar seemed reassured and nodded her head, giving his hand a squeeze. "Jason, Invictius is your father."

Jason was taken aback, and it took a few seconds for his mind to register what Skylar had said. He looked at Diana, she must

CHAPTER TWELVE

have known about this because she remained as calm as a pool of untouched water.

"How?" asked Jason, his mind racing. He had seen the evil in Invictius' eyes. The hatred. Was that monster really his father? His family?

"I know, Jason," said Diana, in an offhand way that was not exactly helpful in this delicate situation. "This is a lot to take in. But don't be angry at Skylar, she wasn't sure what to do."

Jason didn't answer, for he was lost in his own thoughts. Diana's voice faded away and echoed like a call in a tunnel. He dimly heard her words and in his mind he knew he wasn't angry at Skylar. If anything he was relieved, because he knew that if Skylar had told him sooner than he would never have managed to face Invictius, even if it was for the briefest second.

"Jason?"

Skylar's voice rang out amidst Jason's thoughts, and he was brought out of the depths of his mind by the familiar tone, the reassuring voice.

"Jason," said Skylar, lowering her face guiltily. "You have every right to be angry at me. It was wrong of me to keep this from you. I– I just couldn't bear to reveal this terrible truth until..." Skylar's voice faltered as she uttered the last sentence, "until we met Diana."

"What does Diana have to do with this?" asked Jason, glancing at Diana's impassive face. "Why did you tell her before me?"

Skylar took a deep breath in. In the silence that seemed to be suspended between them, Jason could hear Ember's and

Lucinda's excited voices carrying in from the outside world. A world that was so far away in that stifling cave. An understanding passed between Skylar and Diana as they glanced at each other.

"Jason–" began Skylar.

"Can I?" interrupted Diana.

Skylar nodded.

"Jason," said Diana, raising her head to look into Jason's expectant but fearful face. "I'm Skylar's daughter... I'm your cousin."

It took a moment for Jason to register what she had said, then he repeated the words in his mind over and over again. Each time, getting more accustomed to them. Jason almost made himself believe that Diana had been living with him all his life, that they had shared happy and sad times together. He almost made himself believe that he had always known, deep down in his heart, that he had a cousin. Lost, but not broken. A cousin that had undergone vicious and evil experiments. A cousin that was no-doubt the strongest warrior he had ever met.

Jason looked up from the stony floor. He saw in Skylar's lost gaze that she feared his reaction. And a simple glance at Diana clearly showed how hard she was trying not to care.

"I'm happy that you're my cousin," said Jason, smiling at Diana.

Her face flushed with relief, and she threw her arms around him in a warm embrace. Diana laughed with pure joy. Tears were running down her face, happy tears. Joyful tears. Skylar couldn't keep a smile off her face and drew Diana and Jason in her arms.

The joyous noises from within the cave brought Ember and Lucinda from outside. They had no idea what was going on and

CHAPTER TWELVE

their puzzled faces made Jason laugh out loud. Diana hurried away from Skylar and hugged Ember as tight as she could. In seconds, everyone was laughing and celebrating, though Ember and Lucinda had no idea why.

In broken sentences, Diana, Jason and Skylar explained why it was that they were happy. Ember and Lucinda were both shocked at first, but knew that this was the happy truth. Laughter filled the air, and the rest of the day was spent in happiness.

* * *

Jason shifted his weight to get as comfortable as possible on the hard stone. Skylar had wanted to speak to him, the laughter and happiness of the earlier day having faded from her eyes. Now there was just worry and fear.

Jason noticed a thin silhouette coming toward him and stiffened. But soon the figure's details became easier to see. It was Skylar. She put her finger to her lips, signaling to him to be quiet until she arrived at his side.

Once she was close enough to touch, Jason burst out, "Why did you want to talk to me?"

"Shh," said Skylar, sitting down beside him. "It's about Invictius."

"It's all right," said Jason quickly. "I don't hold it against you."

"No, no," said Skylar immediately. "It's not about that. It's about his plans."

Skylar looked expectantly at Jason's moonlit face. For a second the only sound was the rushing of the wind over the high treetops of the forest. The moonlight fell on Jason's face, causing half of it to fall in shadow but making the rest glow like the moon.

"What about his plans?" asked Jason quietly.

"Do you remember what Invictius used to do to Diana?"

"He used to experiment on her," said Jason, shivering at the cruelty of it.

"Yes," said Skylar. "But do you know why?"

"Not really," said Jason, looking up at Skylar again, willing himself to find some sort of clue as to what she would say.

"He wanted to take her power for his own," said Skylar, the old sadness returning to her eyes. "He told me about his great plan, as he put it." Skylar sighed, hesitant to utter the following words. "He wants to take the power of all the Gifted."

"What?" asked Jason, his rapt attention turning to hatred toward Invictius.

"He wants to take their power, so he can defeat you," said Skylar.

"Then we have to stop him," said Jason, practically jumping off the stone in his haste to stop the villain. "We have to find the Gifted before him."

"No, Jason," said Skylar, grabbing hold of his arm. "We can't. It's too dangerous–"

"No, it's not. You're just saying that because you're worried about me. But this time it will be even easier than rescuing you

CHAPTER TWELVE

from Invictius, because we're not falling right into his hands, we'll be keeping one step ahead of him."

"Jason," said Skylar, desperately grabbing hold of his sleeve. "Don't do this. Please, don't do this. I can't let you risk your life just to save their lives. They'll be reborn, they will be fine. Just, please don't do this to me."

Jason stood stock still and utterly silent. He couldn't believe Skylar would stop him. Deep inside Jason knew this was what he should do, he knew this was his destiny. All of a sudden a small, pleading voice echoed in Jason's head.

Don't you owe something to Skylar? said the voice. Shouldn't you stay with her instead of going against her wishes? Would you really break her heart to save the lives of people you don't even know?

I must, replied Jason's conscience. It is my duty to my kind. I am a Gifted. I must protect those like me.

What about Skylar? You would–

With an effort Jason blocked the voice. He knew he didn't need this right now. He didn't need to have his heart and mind fighting against each other. Not now. Jason looked at Skylar. She had the same desperate face as when she had told him about Invictius being his father. Her beautiful features were shadowed with worry and sadness. This did not improve Jason's mood. Skylar's face had been drawn with loss ever since Jason could remember. He supposed a lot of it had to do with Diana, and possibly, Invictius.

"Please," said Skylar, tears coming to her eyes. "Please don't do this."

Skylar's desperation made Jason react.

"I won't," said Jason.

"Thank you," said Skylar, drawing Jason in a hug. "Thank you."

That night was the most tumultuous night in Jason's life. The promise had been hasty and heartfelt. Jason almost wished he hadn't agreed and that Skylar had burst into tears instead. In his uncomfortable, leafy bed, Jason thought of the Gifted that would now be destined to die. As the Keeper, Jason knew he couldn't let that happen. Jason knew he would have to go behind Skylar's back, even if that meant losing her forever.

CHAPTER TWELVE

Epilogue

Invictius walked into the cave, looking around. Once he had determined it was big enough for Xander, he nodded. Dragon Xander limped into the cave. One of the boulders of the mountain had completely crushed one of Xander's legs. Invictius would probably have to heal that later.

Xander snorted in annoyance as he dragged a boy's body into the cave. The boy wasn't dead, though he was close to it. Invictius would have to bind him before the boy woke up.

Xander placed the boy in a corner not too-gently, noted Invictius.

"We are confined to this sty?" snorted Xander.

Invictius' lips pulled back in a sneer. "It is good enough. That boy cannot find us here."

Xander bowed his head, and stared at the ground in anger. "Yes, my lord."

Invictius nodded his head and summoned his staff. With his shadow gifts, he had altered it a bit. The ebony had been mahogany, but the silver traces had always been there and the orb had always been black.

Invictius raised his staff, aiming it at the far corner of the cave. The shadows were summoned, and they melded together to create a throne of darkness. Invictius strode over to it and reposed himself upon it.

He watched the boy, his face expressionless. Xander backed out of the cave without a word, and Invictius didn't bother taking notice of him. Invictius studied the boy. The boy was a Gifted, of course, and perhaps the only thing that had survived the mountain caving in.

The boy's face started to twitch and Invictius smiled in satisfaction. He quickly shielded his mind with a small flick of his wrist. After a moment the boy's eyes snapped open. Invictius calmly called on the shadows, and they curled around the boy, binding him in black coils of darkness.

Invictius stood up, and placed himself so that the boy could see him. The boy's eyes widened in shock, and he opened his mouth. Before the boy could say anything, Invictius flicked his wrist, causing the shadows to cover the boy's mouth as well.

Invictius studied the boy. He had fair, nearly-golden hair. The boy's golden eyes stared at Invictius with hatred, but Invictius took no note of this. The boy was unharmed except for a long gash down the side of his face. Invictius didn't bother healing it. Let the boy keep the scar. He would gain more wounds in his life anyway.

"You are going to be very useful to me, boy," said Invictius with a smile. "I've always wanted the Gifted of mind. Minds are fragile things, easily broken and easily deceived. I warn you not to try and escape. The wolves get very hungry after a chase."

EPILOGUE

The boy shouted something, but it was muffled by the gag of darkness.

Invictius smile. "Don't struggle, Gifted of the mind, after all, your fate is already sealed."

The boy struggled more than ever and shouted something unintelligible.

"Every day that passes shall bring pain," promised Invictius. "When I begin the experiments, your mind may not be your own."

The boy finally fell silent, acknowledging this battle as already lost. Invictius smiled and gestured with his hand. Immediately, the shadows that had bound the boy fell away, vanishing into the darkness.

"You're evil," said the Gifted of mind. "I will never serve you freely."

"Don't worry," said Invictius, reposing himself upon his throne of darkness. "I don't need you to. But you will help me and your gifts will be mine. My son's defeat will be so sweet."

A WORD TO THE READER

LIST OF REALMS

The World of Wizards: A Realm filled with magic and wonder and spells.

The Realm of Sorcerers: A Realm where people with a single power reside. They are similar to Gifted, but their powers are different.

The Realm of Magic: This is the Realm where magic is from. It is one of the first Realms founded.

Nolman's Realm: This Realm is where most Nolman's live and where Jason is from.

21st century: This Realm is called this because it is currently in the 21st century. Most of my readers should currently be in this Realm.

Mid-Evil: Mid-Evil is the original birthplace of evil. The Bermuda Triangle is here as well as in the 21st century.

Futura: This Realm is a place filled with technology and innovation.

Acknowledgments

I would like to thank my family, of course, but specifically my oldest sister Elizabeth. She edited as much as she could and inspired me to write it. She's supported me so much this year and, if she can find some time while being a doctor, will read some of my following books.

I'd also like to thank my second-oldest sister, Sarah. She's supported me with the writing of this book, and I'm even dedicating the first book of another series I'm writing to her.

Printed in Great Britain
by Amazon